I0725971

THE DILF

A TEMPERANCE FALLS ROMANCE

LONDON HALE

the DILF

LONDON HALE

Copyright © 2017 by London Hale

All rights reserved

No part of this book may be reproduced in any form or by any electronic or mechanical means, including information storage and retrieval systems, without written permission from the author, except for the use of brief quotations in a book review.

The DILF is a work of fiction. Names, characters, places, and incidents are either the products of the author's imagination or are used fictitiously, and any resemblances to actual persons, living or dead, business establishments, events, or locales is coincidental.

Edited by Lisa Hollett of Silently Correcting Your Grammar, LLC

Cover Art © Brighton Walsh

Digital ISBN: 978-1-944336-25-7

Paperback ISBN: 978-1-944336-26-4

For inquiries, contact London Hale at london@londonhale.com

LONDON HALE

*To our husbands,
who showed us exactly how hot DILFs can be.*

chapter one

BRANDON

THERE WAS SOMETHING disturbing about walking into a hospital when your reasons for being there were completely in the wrong. Still, I did it. Climbed out of my car after rushing across town, all because of a phone call. I'd seen this sort of nonsense on dramatic television shows—the whole one moment changes your life bullshit. But I guess it wasn't bullshit, not really. Should have been. Would have been, but then I'd spent an evening with someone I shouldn't have been alone with, and as cliché as it sounded, my world changed. My focus changed. In all the wrong ways.

So when the phone rang and the news that Lara McKay—mother of my daughter's best friend—was in a horrible accident, that new focus sent me scurrying to find out what I could do to help. But again, for the wrong reasons.

Yes, Lara was hurt. Yes, she needed someone to check on her since she had no family here except her daughter. Yes, my being her daughter's best friend's father gave me access to more of her life than a casual acquaintance, so I felt comfortable coming when I found out about the accident. That was all fine. What wasn't fine was the reason I chose to come to the hospital—because it wasn't Lara.

It was her daughter.

Genesis.

One of the sexiest human beings I'd ever had the unfortunate luck to come across. Fiery, wild, bold—Gen wasn't a woman you could ignore. Especially not when she turned those huge blue eyes on you. It was impossible. Until you remembered she was eighteen years old. Then…not so impossible. Hard for sure, just as she made me every time she looked my way, but not impossible.

Yet there I was, storming into the hospital because I knew she'd be alone. I knew she'd need someone. And I wanted that someone to be me.

"Lara McKay," I said as soon as I approached the information desk. The man behind it, who wore an obnoxiously decorated sticker with the name Paul in the middle of it, frowned and typed, frowned and typed. Slowly. If he'd been an employee of mine, I'd have fired him already. And that was before he started humming to himself.

"Car accident," I said, doing my best not to grit my teeth. "Came in through the emergency room."

He nodded and pressed a few more buttons at the

pace of a sloth. "Got it. Looks like she's in the surgical ward. Are you family?"

"Yes, I am." The lie came easily—too easily—but the fact that my own cousin was a surgeon here had taught me a few things. Like that only family was allowed in the surgical waiting room, and that the volunteers behind the desk would never ask for proof of relationship.

Paul did not disappoint. "Perfect. Okay, here's a guest badge. Please wear it throughout the hospital. Surgery is up on—"

"Four," I said, cutting him off as I snatched the plastic badge from his fingers. "Yeah, I got it. Thanks."

I rushed to the elevators and jabbed the up button more times than necessary. The damn thing seemed to take forever to arrive and even longer for the doors to slide closed behind me. What was it with this place and obstacles?

As I stared at the lights telling me what floor we were on, my impatience burned hot under my skin, my need to get upstairs harsh and painful. I would've liked to have said it was for Lara. She was a nice lady, pretty and sexy. Between her looks, her charm, and the fact that we were the youngest parents on the PTA—fully a decade younger than the rest—it would have made sense for us to date. Hell, we'd even flirted a bit when the girls first met and we started seeing each other at playdates and birthday parties. Two single people in their early twenties trying to navigate the waters of being a parent and an adult tended to gravitate together. But no, she wasn't for me. No one had been, really.

I'd kept any romantic connections private—very private. Temperance Falls was a small island with big eyes and even bigger ears. The last thing I needed was to start dating someone and risk my reputation. I had a little girl to raise, one I protected with everything I had. Lara had been barely more than a blip on my attraction screen.

Her daughter was a whole different story, and I was going to end up in hell for the thoughts I'd had about her. Those thoughts—fantasies, if I was being honest—had started recently. Really recently. Just since the night barely over a week ago, when she'd sat on my couch talking with me as if we were old friends. Leg up and tucked beneath her, far too much skin on display, red hair tumbling over her shoulders— she'd been a dream come true. A siren calling to the basest parts of me. And smart. The girl was charming, personable, witty…and sex on legs. I'd barely been able to resist her; the only thing keeping me from pinning her under me was the knowledge that my own daughter, Gen's best friend, had been sleeping upstairs at the time. That and the fact that she was far too young for me. Probably.

Think of the devil, and he shall appear…

"Brandon." Genesis caught me as I stepped off the elevator, those killer eyes meeting mine. They were so bloodshot, so pained, so worried. I couldn't help myself. I grabbed the girl and pulled her into a hug, shielding her as much as I could with my body.

"Are you okay?" I asked, nearly shaking with my need to press myself against her. To feel more of those curves. To hold her tight and never let her go so I didn't have to think about what would have happened if she'd been in the same car as her mom when it went over the bridge. Fuck, she wasn't mine in any way, but that would have killed me.

Gen clutched my shoulders, her delicate fingers pressing deep, and nodded against my chest. "I'm fine. My mom's bad, though. There's swelling around her brain, plus her leg's pretty mangled. I don't… I'm not sure what we're going to do."

The fear in her voice gutted me. "It's okay. It'll be okay."

A silent moment, the feel of her body melting into mine, and then she cried. Hard. Fuck, that wasn't like Gen. The girl was loud, brash, and audacious. Sexy in a way that stopped men in their tracks. I'd done a good job of ignoring those facts as she grew into them, but then last week, after Evie's graduation party… I couldn't ignore them anymore. And I hated myself for thinking about that while she sobbed in my arms. Asshole of the Year award, well deserved.

A polite cough had me turning, though I didn't let go of Gen. I kept her wrapped up and safe. Close to me.

"Hey, Brandon." My cousin stood before me looking tired and slightly curious. Of course, he did—I had a sexy-as-fuck eighteen-year-old in my arms. Shit.

"Josh. Good to see you." I reached out a hand, moving Gen into my side so our embrace looked a little more appropriate. Which was fine so long as no one noticed the massive fucking hard-on I was now sporting. "How's Lara doing?"

"She's hanging in. Her lower left leg is broken in three places, and her MCL is completely torn. We have the best orthopedic surgery team on their way in to take care of that, but it's not our priority." He glanced at Gen, who was still tucked against me with her hand on my chest. "Your mom took a pretty solid hit to the head, and that's the issue we need to address immediately. There's a lot of swelling, and that can cause brain damage, but this isn't a touch-and-go situation. We'll relieve the pressure by opening up a flap in her skull and keep her unconscious for a few days to give her brain time to heal."

Gen felt rigid in my arms, so I jumped in with the first question I needed answered. "So, you're operating today. When will they operate on her leg?"

"The team should be here tomorrow."

The single parent in me couldn't help but ask, "And what's her recovery timeline?"

Josh held my gaze, his concern obvious. "Minimum two weeks in the hospital, then another two to six in rehab. It depends on the amount of damage—if any—to her brain."

Four weeks minimum. Gen could end up alone, without someone to look over her, for a month. In the back of my mind, I knew she didn't need another person around, but that didn't appease the instinctual part of me that didn't want her unprotected.

"Okay." Gen pulled away from me before I could decide what to do about the four-week thing, squaring her shoulders, a little of that fire back in her eyes. "When can I see her?"

Josh frowned, shooting a look my way before refocusing on the woman before him. "You can see her now, but only for a few minutes. I want her in an operating room within the hour."

"Fine. Let's go." Gen snatched her bag off a chair, then reached as if to grab my hand. Looking somewhat lost. Somewhat vulnerable. Looking as if she needed me. "Come with me?"

Fuck, the dirty places my brain went when she said that, when she looked at me like that. How could I possibly tell her no?

"Of course."

We followed Josh to a room off the main hallway. The place was dim, almost dark, but not enough that we couldn't see the woman huddled under the sheet. Couldn't see the bruises and cuts, the pillow-like device holding her leg in place. Gen stiffened when she walked in, completely froze for a moment as she took in the sight of her mother so damaged. I squeezed her hand and hoped my presence offered at least a modicum of comfort.

"Five minutes," Josh whispered as he caught my eye. "I'll talk to you later?"

I nodded, knowing that talk would be about why I was touching a young girl who wasn't my daughter. Shit, a woman. I needed to remember that. Gen was eighteen.

Just like my daughter.

Who was fucking my best friend.

When had my life become a soap opera?

"Mom," Gen whispered, leaning over the bed. I stayed back, kept out of the way. Gave the two ladies their space. Lara's eyes fluttered a few times before finally opening, focusing in on her daughter immediately.

"Gen." Her voice was rough, pained. Too quiet. "You okay?"

Gen huffed a laugh. "You were the one in a car accident, but you're asking if I'm okay?"

"It's the mom in me. I can't help myself."

"I'm fine. How are you?"

"I feel like I got hit by a semitruck and fell off a bridge. Oh wait, I did."

"Mom, be serious."

"Fine. I feel like ass. Everything hurts, even focusing my eyes."

"The doctor's going to fix you."

"I know." She licked her lips, glancing my way. "Brandon, can you take her?"

My eyes darted to Gen before returning to the patient. "Lara?"

"I don't want her home alone for days on end. Can you take her? Let her come stay with you and Evie?"

Temptation had a way of making you do things you shouldn't. Wrong things. I should have told Lara that Evie no longer lived with me. That maybe Gen staying with me—the man who had jacked off to thoughts of her every day for the past week—wouldn't be a good idea. The right thing would have been not to lust after a teenager.

I did not do the right thing.

"Of course. Gen can stay with me as long as she'd like."

Gen stiffened, her shoulders going tight as she glanced back at me, then addressed her mother. "Mom, no. I can stay at home by myself. I'm almost nineteen. I don't need a handler."

"I know you don't, but I'd feel better if I knew you were taken care of." She flicked her eyes in my direction, and my guilt multiplied. "Otherwise, I'm just going to be in here, worrying about you."

The fight in Gen went out as soon as her mom spoke the words. "Fine. But promise the only thing you'll think about while you're in here is getting better."

"I promise. I know Brandon will take good care of you."

Yeah, I would. Hopefully without letting her know how much her curvy little body turned me on. How hard it was for me not to reach out and touch every inch of her pale skin. How fucking hard she made me every single day.

There was no denying it. I was going to hell. One I created for myself.

chapter two

GENESIS

TIME WAS IRRELEVANT in the hospital. Minutes flew by in the blink of an eye and simultaneously crawled at the pace of a snail. Evie had come and gone, just checking in to make sure I had everything I needed. Harper, my boss, had even poked in to see if I wanted her to grab me something to eat. But Brandon had put all their worries to rest, practically shooing them out the door. He hadn't left my side since the minute he'd stormed out of the elevator, panic and worry written all over his face. I just wasn't sure if that panic and worry had been for me or my mom.

Hours had passed by the time we got the report from the surgeon that my mom had made it out of surgery okay and that everything had gone as expected. She'd be in a medically induced coma for a few days to help her heal. That thought terrified me, but the surgeon had assured me it was standard.

"You look exhausted," Brandon said, frowning. It seemed like he'd been doing that any time I'd glanced his way. When he'd tried to get me to eat and I'd managed only a couple bites—frowned. When he'd grabbed me a coffee that I hadn't drunk—frowned. When he'd watched me as I talked with the surgeon—frowned. He grabbed my bag off the chair. "Let's get you home."

Except *home* was no longer on the agenda.

If I weren't so shaken from this whole day, I might have been spending more time thinking about what an epically fucking awful idea it was for me to stay at his house. With*out* Evie, since she no longer called her childhood house home, and instead, was shacking up with her superhot, way older boyfriend.

I glanced at Brandon, nodding as I grabbed my bag from him and let him lead me to the elevator, his hand a light touch on my back.

"You want to stop and get something to eat at the diner? You hardly touched your sandwich."

I shook my head. "I'm not hungry."

The thought that the accident could've gone a dozen different ways, all with my mom dying, shook me to my core. My mom was my only family, and it'd always been just her and me. She was so young when she had me; some days it felt like I lived with my best friend rather than my mother.

Some days—when our schedules clashed completely—it felt like I lived alone. On those days,

I'd go over to Evie's house, just for the company. I couldn't stand extended periods of being by myself. It wasn't that I hated my own company—it was more that I *thrived* on the energy of other people. Being with others kept me revitalized and happy. Something my mom knew, which was no doubt why she'd pushed me to stay at Evie's house while she recovered in the hospital.

"How about a candy bar?" Brandon said. "Or I can swing by a drive-thru—whatever you want."

"No thanks."

There was the frown again, this time as we walked out of the hospital and toward the parking lot. Without question, without even discussing the fact that I'd definitely be leaving my car behind—honestly, I didn't particularly want to drive right then anyway—Brandon ushered me toward his Audi, opening the passenger's door for me. I slid inside and stared out the front window, unmoving as he walked around and got in on his side.

"Genesis?"

"Hmm?" I glanced over at him in time to see his forehead crinkle with concern.

He reached across the divide between us and brushed a strand of hair back from my face, then leaned forward, coming so close his mouth nearly touched mine. His breath ghosted over my lips, his eyes studying mine, his heat washing over me. And there it was—that chemistry that had sparked to life only a week ago. He reached around me, but I couldn't pay attention to what he was doing, too focused on his blue—almost gray, they were so light—eyes. How they studied me as if trying to solve something.

"What are you doing?" I whispered.

"Seat belt," he said just as softly before he pulled back, clicking the belt into place.

How I could be so worried for my mom and feel so *alive* at the same time, I didn't know. I'd never experienced anything like it before, didn't know if it was to be expected. Something totally normal. Or if it was something else entirely.

He turned away from me, starting the car as if none of that had happened. As if I hadn't nearly leaned forward to find out what his lips would feel like against mine. As if my nipples weren't hard as stone beneath my shirt. Blowing out a breath, I stared out my window, certain if my mom had half an inkling about the kinds of things I'd thought about doing with Evie's dear old dad, she wouldn't have pushed me to stay with him.

I'd always known Brandon was hot, in a vague, *Wow, your dad is totally a DILF, Evie,* kind of way. It was something I liked to tease her about, but that was all it had been—teasing.

And then that night had happened.

The night of Evie's graduation party—a mere week ago—when she'd needed my help to distract him while she finally went after Nate. I'd figured I'd do my due diligence as a best friend and suffer through an evening with her father to help her out. Turned out, there hadn't been much suffering done.

For the first time in as long as I could remember,

Brandon had laughed. And when he laughed, the whole room stilled. His entire face lit up, the small lines around his eyes crinkling. Then he'd talked to me. More than the way guys usually conversed with me—as a means to an end, only interested in getting in my pants. Brandon had talked to me like I was a person. Like he cared about what I had to say. Like it'd *mattered* to him.

Our apartment was all the way across the island from the hospital—which wasn't saying much considering how tiny the island was. In no time at all, Brandon had the car parked along the curb and was at my side, opening my door before I could finish unbuckling my seat belt and grabbing my things. He followed silently behind me, no question on if he'd come up with me, waiting as I swung open the main door. His hand caught it above my head, holding it open for me as he gestured me inside ahead of him. I tried not to get distracted by the feel of him so close, how the scent of him surrounded me. Tried and failed. I wanted to turn back, bury my face in his chest, and inhale.

"Thanks," I murmured, focusing on just getting up the steps to the apartment and not doing something with my best friend's father that I absolutely shouldn't do.

"Anytime."

My shadow, formerly known as Evie's father, followed me into the apartment, through the small dining area and living room, down the short hallway, not stopping until he was a foot into my bedroom.

I needed some space. I needed him closer. "I'm not going to escape out the window, you know."

He stared at me for a moment, then with his voice a husky murmur, he said, "I just want you safe, Genesis."

I could only blink at him, unable to comprehend what he meant by that. My brain was fried from the long day and the overabundance of emotions flooding my senses. Figuring my best bet was not to comment at all, I shook my head to clear it then grabbed a bag.

I ignored his presence as best I could while I quickly packed—shorts, a few shirts, a pair of jeans—but I couldn't help wondering what he was seeing when he looked around my space. Did it look like a little girl's room? I didn't think so. It was bright and vibrant, the walls painted a deep plum. My room wasn't big—just big enough for a bed and a nightstand, my dresser placed in my closet to save space—but it felt like home to me. The focal point of the room was my bed, just a full-size, but it had a mound of jewel-toned pillows decorating it, and a lavender mosquito net hung from the ceiling at the top.

As I stuffed a couple bras and a handful of colorful lace panties in my bag—Jesus, why didn't I own any plain nude or white underwear?—I willed myself not to look at him. But, of course, I lost the battle. I glanced up to find him staring at the blood-red panties I was in the process of tossing in my bag. His focus was enough to still my action, my hand halting with the scrap of red lace still dangling between my fingers. At the pause, he lifted his gaze to me, and the look in his eyes nearly took my breath away.

Hunger. That was the only way to describe it.

I didn't think it could get any more feral, and then he slid his attention to my bed, to the mound of pillows, his eyes seeming to catalog every square inch of it. And, if possible, his gaze grew even hungrier, his jaw ticking as he stared.

And then he blinked, the tension in the air evaporating, and it was like I'd just come out of a dream.

He cleared his throat, then turned toward the doorway. "I'll just wait for you in the living room. Take all the time you need."

If my nipples hadn't been pebbled under my shirt, my chest flushed from his attention, I'd have sworn I imagined it all. But I hadn't... The way my body was singing was proof enough of that.

I wasn't a stranger to the attention of men. When my boobs decided to show up at fourteen, so did the guys. I'd been the participant in some awkward back seat fumbling, then some not-so-awkward fumbling, then some straight-up good sex. But I'd never, not once, been looked at the way Brandon had just looked at me. Like he could inhale me through his eyes. Like he'd *starve* if he didn't get a taste.

Seemed I wasn't the only one who'd had a change of heart over the past week. It looked like we had some things to discuss. And, well, if exploring whatever this was between Brandon and me was a good way to get my mind off my mom, all the better.

———

Evie's house felt empty without her in it. I'd always known it was big, of course, but it had never really registered. Our laughter and fun had filled up all the empty places inside, making it seem more like a home than a museum. But now, with Evie's things gone, her room not empty, but *bare*, it was different. It felt cold and unwelcoming, and I hated it.

I hated even more how Brandon had shut down after that moment in my bedroom. He'd barely looked at me as we'd left my apartment, and now, he was stiff as a board, his shoulders rigid and his back straight as he led me down the hall past Evie's room and to another bedroom. *Not* his.

"Since it might be a few weeks that you'll be here, I thought you'd feel most comfortable in the guest room instead of Evie's. It has its own bathroom."

Like an attached bathroom was what I needed to feel comfortable. Had he even noticed the tiny closet-sized one my mom and I shared?

"And, um, Ursula, the maid, comes on Tuesdays." He glanced up at me but didn't hold eye contact. "In the afternoon, in case you'll be around then."

"I work all day on Tuesday, so I won't be here." I sailed past him and dropped my bag on the bed, wanting—*needing*—to see if the reaction he'd had at my apartment was all in my head. I had the strangest urge to yank out those lace bras and panties and… *taunt* him with them. I didn't know what this pull between us was, but I wasn't questioning it.

Before I could get the bag unzipped, before I could grab any of the offending garments, he coughed then mumbled good night, and it sounded like he'd bumped into the wall in his haste to leave. I turned my gaze in his direction just as the door closed behind him, the soft click of the latch echoing like a gunshot in the otherwise silent room.

And then it was just me. Alone in this too big house, without anyone to keep me company. In fact, I was pretty sure I'd just run off my only reprieve from isolation.

God, I probably had misread the tension in my apartment. On top of everything I'd had to deal with today, I now had the bitter taste of humiliation to add to the too-long list.

My shoulders sagged, the weight of the day bearing down on me, and I closed my eyes. I was exhausted, having spent hours at the hospital, fear and uncertainty and tension my only companions. If I'd lost Mom… God, I couldn't even stand to finish the thought.

But she was going to be fine. The doctor—what was his name?—had said so. It'd take a lot of therapy, and she'd be in pain in the interim, but she'd be fine eventually.

With that thought comforting me, I mindlessly got ready for bed, changing into my tank top and boy shorts, before brushing my teeth in the en suite bathroom. I tried not to think about the events of the day as I pulled my mop of hair up on top of my head, securing it in a messy bun with an elastic before flipping the light switch to bathe the room in darkness. I stumbled my way toward the bed, hating the new space I'd only been in once before, years ago. Hating how isolating it felt. Brushing aside the gnawing in my stomach, I slipped under the covers and stared at the ceiling, listening to absolute silence. The loneliness almost crushing me.

chapter three

RED. My entire world suddenly revolved around red. Red hair, red lips, and red fucking panties. Lacy and nearly see-through, they'd hung from Gen's fingers like a cape in front of a bull. Teasing me. Egging me on to…what? Throw her on that purple bed and fuck that sweet, young pussy? Was that where my attraction was headed? It certainly seemed that way when we'd stood in her little bedroom, a pair of deep red panties making everything in the world disappear except the need to find out what they looked like on the woman holding them.

Walking out of her bedroom had been one of the hardest things I'd ever done, and not just because the sight of those panties had turned my cock to motherfucking steel. No, the mental part was harder to deal with. Convincing myself to stay strong against the pull. Even when those panties—those hot, red calling cards of sex—had been practically waved in my face, I'd resisted. It'd been a long fucking time since I'd done anything more than the most cursory of sex acts. Walking out of that room should have earned me a damn gold medal in control.

I'd run away from Gen, needing space, giving myself time to calm the fuck down. And I was still running. Hiding, really. In my own house. I was also far too sober considering how long my day had been. It was time to change a few of those facts.

I crept out of my bedroom, regretting walking out the door as soon as I took a single step. Trouble was coming; I could feel it. But there was no way I was sleeping yet. Not with red constantly dancing behind my eyes and making my hands itch to touch. I swear, the girl in the guest room had purposely teased me by picking the brightest, most intriguing panties in her drawer. Never mind the other bits of lace and satin I had noticed as well. I never should have followed her into her bedroom. Shit, I never should have agreed to let her stay with me without Evie home as a buffer. But that ship had sailed.

I headed straight to my office on the first floor, needing the whiskey I kept there. I figured I was safe in my own home seeing as it was well past midnight, but I was wrong. So very wrong. I poured a whiskey into a rocks glass and took a sip before it hit me. Sounds. Someone else was awake. I should have ignored the temptation, but it was impossible, so I followed the sounds, curiosity a heavy yoke around my neck. The television was on in the back family room, the soft blue light pulling me in. Dragging me back there. To the only person who could have been watching.

Gen looked up the second I walked in the room, and my goddamn cock betrayed me at the sight. She was half naked, wearing only a thin tank top and some sort of tiny, tight shorts. What was she trying to do? Kill me? Did she not understand how long her legs looked in those things? How her full breasts pushed at the ridiculous fabric of her top? How much I wanted to bury my face between her legs and see just how soft those shorts were?

As she stared at me, waiting me out, I took a sip of my whiskey to resettle my thoughts.

"You're up late," I said when I pulled the glass away from my lips. The burn felt good, calming. Made me feel invincible to the seductress on my couch.

The woman—girl, just a girl—looked at me like I was something on the menu. My invincibility went up in flames with a single once-over. She didn't stop until she'd dragged her eyes all the way down my body and halfway back up. Stopping quite noticeably on my very hard, very needful cock.

"It was too quiet. I couldn't sleep."

I nodded when she finally forced those eyes back to mine, swallowing another sip of whiskey merely as a distraction. I should have left. I should have turned around and run back to my room. I should have been a responsible adult, but I couldn't. Gen looked so small as she sat in the dark with light from the television bathing her features. I couldn't leave her like that.

"What are you watching?" I approached slowly, giving myself time to calm the fuck down.

"*Gilmore Girls*, my mom's favorite." She shrugged and flicked her eyes to the screen. "It's dumb, but it makes me feel closer to her."

"Can't say I've ever seen an episode," I said as I took the seat next to Gen. I wanted to be a better man and give her space, but the whiskey tasted too good and she looked too delicate for me to stay far away. Lonely, almost. I knew that feeling, knew it well. I'd committed myself to raising Evie after her mother left, which meant keeping all relationships at the friend level, never letting a woman into my life who could upset my daughter, and working myself to the bone to take care of her. Loneliness had hounded my ass for almost two decades. But I wasn't alone right then, and neither was Gen.

I licked my lips as she moved closer, noticing the shiver that seemed to crawl up her body. "Are you cold?"

"Yeah. It's a little chilly down here."

I reached behind her for the blanket hanging along the back of the couch. "Here."

"Thanks." She pulled the fabric around her, covering herself from my greedy eyes, thank fuck. But then she tossed one side over my lap. Joining the two of us. Even moving closer so we could both be covered.

"What are you doing?"

"Sharing. Like you should be."

"And what is it I should be sharing?"

"Whatever you've got in that glass."

I coughed and shook my head, holding the glass closer to my mouth as I readied for another sip. "You're too young."

"I'm old enough to vote, get married, and have sex with whomever I want. I'm not that young anymore, Brandon."

Her words—her blunt, accurate words—made my cock twitch. I shifted on the seat, unable not to turn at least a few inches toward her. To look into that face and see her pride, her strength, her independence. "You're right. You're not that young anymore, Genesis. But I'm still not giving it to you."

She positively smirked, those eyes of hers going wicked, and I knew I'd made a mistake with my word choice. The possibilities of what I meant by "it" hung between us, weighty and meaningful. It could have been anything—the whiskey, a kiss, my cock. I wasn't giving her anything but my attention, yet I wanted to. Wanted to so badly, I knew I'd be jacking off to this memory all fucking week. Knew I'd be hard every second I was in my own home simply because she'd been there as well. Hell, I almost looked forward to it.

No person had intrigued me as much as Gen did in almost twenty years. As dirty and wrong as I was, I still wanted her. Wanted to get her on her back and find out how wet I could make her. How much she'd tremble under my hands and mouth. Gen didn't seem like the sort of girl who'd waited. She had a confidence about her, a sensuality born of comfort around members of the opposite sex. As much as I hated knowing she'd given herself to others, I liked it, too. I wanted to show them up. Show her how a real man could take care of her pussy. I wanted to make her come until only my name fell from those cock-sucking lips.

Staring into her eyes, I took a sip of my whiskey, swirling the dark liquid as I pulled the glass away. My own cape hanging before the bull. My turn to tease.

Gen's eyes stayed locked on mine, ignoring the glass. Or so I thought. "You're really not going to give me a taste?"

Yes. I'd give her everything. All of me. Every fucking inch over and over. "No."

She curled her legs under her, rising slightly onto her knees. Looking me square in the eyes as she leaned closer. "What if I come take it?"

Fuck me. I couldn't resist that voice, that look on her face. That refusal to back down. I dropped a hand to her hip as she leaned across me, and I kept my mouth shut. She locked her eyes on mine as she pressed her breasts to my arm and stretched. Her scent surrounded me, and the warmth of her skin scorched across mine. I was completely under her spell, at her mercy.

With a swipe of her tongue to her bottom lip, she took the glass from my hand. I was helpless to resist her, so I let her grab my drink. Let her wrap her fingers around mine and pull the glass right from my hand. My cock practically wept as my now empty hand found its way to her shoulder, as she brought the glass to her lips and took a sip. And motherfucking hell, did I long for my tongue to follow that whiskey past her lips. I needed to taste her, to know how Gen and the smoke of whiskey went together. I needed, and goddammit, I couldn't keep resisting.

I rubbed my thumb along her collarbone, unable to deny the feel of her skin against mine. "Good?"

I wasn't sure if I was asking about my touch or the drink, but Gen didn't disappoint in her answer. She rolled closer, her face barely an inch from mine as she set the glass on the end table. My hand on her shoulder dropped lower, my thumb brushing over the swell of her breast.

She sighed and closed her eyes for a moment. "So fucking good."

"Gen." My voice sounded hoarse even to my own ears. I wanted to fight the desire within me, the need to touch. Wanted to rip my hand from her hip and her breast and be a better man by heading back to my bedroom where I could jack off alone. But I couldn't. And by the way Gen moved into my touch, forcing my hand down so my thumb rolled over her hard nipple, she didn't want me to either.

"Brandon," she said, her voice a husky whisper. She tugged the blanket around us, wrapping us in a cocoon of darkness and warmth. An intimate little bubble where it was just the two of us.

I leaned forward, brushing my lips against her collarbone, tugging her tank top up until her bare breasts were exposed to me. Needing to see every piece of her. Surrendering to the dark and the heat and the girl. I flicked my tongue along her skin and breathed her in, almost moaning at the sweetness of her. The flavor was a tease, a light and airy bit of almost sugary goodness. It appeased nothing, though. I wanted to taste more, to lick every inch. To spread her legs and devour her. I wanted to demand she lie back and let me make her come, but she beat me to the demanding part.

Gen rocked forward, letting her lips brush against my ear. "You need to kiss me."

She was right, so I did. I slid the hand on her hip up to cradle her head, tightening the other against her breast. Without breaking from the moment, I pulled her into me. Against me. Practically on top of me. My lips found hers a moment later, and I didn't wait. I took. Not a slow, sweet first kiss. Not a careful, awkward one either. No, I kissed her like a man who wanted to own her. Kissed her hard and deep from the get-go, pulled her to straddle my lap, and devoured those fucking lips that had teased me for a week. She kissed me back just as hard, just as rough. The taste of whiskey on her tongue was even more of a treat for me. More of a turn-on. And when her hot, soft pussy landed on my cock as she straddled me, even with our clothing between us, I knew I was done.

"Gen." I ground against her, taking. Too much taking. I didn't want to take from Gen. She deserved more, deserved better. I wanted to give. So I twisted just enough to open her up wider, and I picked her up. She gasped and gripped my shoulders as if afraid I'd somehow drop her, that I'd let her go. She had no idea how far off she was from what I wanted to do.

I pressed the small of her back against the arm of the couch, keeping one hand behind her shoulders for support, letting the blanket shield us from the outside world. Holding her up as I kept her knees spread. Those tiny shorts became my nemesis, the fabric pulled taut across her pussy, the shadows too deep for me to see anything else. Didn't matter—I was about to feel. I could save the looking for another night.

I moved closer, inching higher as I tucked a knee beneath me, licking along her collarbone once more. She tasted so sweet, so irresistible. So mine.

I slid a hand up her thigh, right into her panties and along the underside of that full, luscious ass. I wanted to grab it, smack it, bite it, but that would be for me. Only me. This was for Gen. I worked my hand farther, loving the way she relaxed as I teased the seam of her thigh, the way her hot little breaths burst against my forehead with every inch. She clung to my shoulder, one leg against the back of the couch, the other dangling off the edge. Open. Willing. Ready.

Finally, warm and wet met my fingers, and I groaned. "So fucking soft."

Gen shuddered as I brushed a knuckle over her clit before sliding back down, her moan long and loud in our private blanket fort. Her hips jerked, then she stilled, breaths still heavy, body on edge. I wanted to push her over that. To watch her become nothing more than sensation and reaction. I wanted to make her scream.

"Ride me," I whispered. I rose a little higher,

changed the angle of my hand against her pussy, needing a taste so badly I could hardly breathe. "I want to feel you come all over my hand."

Gen groaned as I licked over her nipple. Grabbed my hair as I sucked on it. Legs spread, half held up by the arm of the couch, head thrown back and her tiny clothes in total disarray, she was the ultimate temptation.

And I was giving in.

"You like my mouth on you? Or do you like my fingers better?" I bit her nipple, sucking harder as I teased her pussy with two fingers. Rubbing, stroking, biting, moaning all at once. She jerked and hissed, arching her back and rocking those hips over me. Just what I wanted her to do. "You have no idea how much I want to taste you, Genesis. Every inch. You're so fucking wet right now, aren't you? I can feel it. I want to bury my face in that sweet pussy and lap up every drop."

Gen groaned, spreading her legs farther. "Oh God, do it."

Fuck, I wanted to. But I knew if I got her naked I wouldn't just be eating that pussy. I'd fuck her. I'd be unable to resist the draw of what I knew was going to be a tight, hot heaven, and I'd be inside her within seconds. So I resisted. Mostly.

I slid a single finger in deep instead, nearly coming in my goddamned pajama pants at how tight she was. Rocking harder, keeping the side of my thumb against her clit, I added a second finger, stretching her, wishing I could fill her with my cock. I let the blanket fall a little, let the blue light from the television shine on her. I wanted to see her come, needed it. Focusing solely on her pleasure even as my cock soaked a spot on my pajama pants. Didn't matter—this was about her. About my Genesis.

"Come on me," I said, pressing deeper, harder. Working her faster. She leaned back, arching her body, grabbing hold of one of her tits as she moaned and gasped. Close, so close. Her. Me. Her body swaying was practically hypnotic, the friction it caused almost enough to make me come for her. Under her. With her. Fuck, she was so beautiful, so warm and soft. So fucking sensuous. I couldn't resist. I added a third finger, letting her adjust to the width, knowing my cock would be wider. She took it all, arching, rocking, and jerking as she hit the point of no return.

Gen threw her head back and moaned without holding back as she came. She was beautiful in that moment. So gorgeous, I almost lost all my control. The flush on her chest, the way she gripped her breast and bit her lip as she shook. Beautiful. Sexy. Hottest fucking thing I'd ever seen in my life. The blanket fell to the floor, baring every inch of her to me. Disheveled and debauched, sitting astride my lap, the hard ridge in my own pants obscene against her tiny shorts.

The ache in my cock grew deeper as I took her in, more painful. I wanted to slide inside her, wanted to fill her with myself, wanted to watch her ride me. Watch my cock disappear inside her. I wanted to fuck her more than I wanted to breathe, but when she came down, when she smiled up at me as if I'd done something amazing for her, she no longer looked like a wanton temptress. She looked…young.

Fuck, this girl was the same age as my daughter.

I grabbed her wrist as she stroked my cock over my pajama pants, unable to get that thought off my mind. "Stop, Gen."

"What's wrong?"

I shook my head, feeling sick. My gut twisting and burning as I pulled my hand from her shorts. "We can't."

"Can't what?"

I pushed her to the side and stood, adjusting myself through my pants. "I'm sorry, but we can't do that. I shouldn't have pushed you like I did."

"Pushed me?" she said, her voice shocked and possibly a little pissed, neither what I'd been going for.

"I'm sorry. It won't happen again." I headed for the hallway, needing to get away from the temptress behind me. "It might be best if we both get some sleep."

"Brandon, what—"

"Goodnight, Gen."

And I left. Feeling like a coward and a thief. Feeling like I'd just messed everything up, though whether it was from what we'd done or how I'd left, I had no idea.

chapter four

GENESIS

IT WAS NEARLY noon before I woke up the next morning, the house still and silent around me, just like it had been until the early morning hours when the exhaustion had finally overcome me, and I'd fallen asleep. Confused, turned on, and…hurt.

There was no denying the fissure of pain that had crept in last night as I'd watched Brandon run out of the family room and away from me, like I was a succubus there to seduce him into giving me his soul.

Turned out, that hurt wasn't going to go away with a few hours of sleep. Not when it was clear Brandon was gone, and I was all alone in the house. It didn't take a genius to figure out he'd fled, probably at the crack of dawn, the very minute it would've been acceptable to arrive at the office. Though fled may have been too strong of a word. It was a weekday, and he had a job to go to. Maybe it was just like any other day, and he was merely getting a jump-start on his workday.

Right. His bailing had absolutely nothing to do with what we'd experienced together on the couch.

I'd never been a very good liar—to others or myself. Wore too much of my heart on my sleeve. I didn't have time for bullshit, wasn't interested in it, and I gave the same courtesy to others. I was pretty sure Brandon would've gone straight to the office after he'd practically sprinted from the family room, if doing so wouldn't have been considered impolite. Didn't matter that it had been one in the morning. I'd seen it in his eyes—all that mattered had been getting away from what had happened. Getting away from *me*.

And wasn't that just an awesome new low I'd hit? Running someone out of their own house? Jesus. I knew I came on strong sometimes—had that been what happened last night? It wouldn't have been the first time.

As of ten days ago, I hadn't even given Brandon a second thought. Of course, I'd liked watching him hang out at the pool in his backyard, all that muscled perfection on display. But I'd liked it just as I liked checking out Instagram models—they were pretty to look at, nice to get my daily fill of eye candy, but nothing would ever come of that attraction.

And now…now, I couldn't keep my mind off him. The funny thing was, the part of our interaction that had made me sit back and see him—really *see* him—for the first time had been the way he'd talked to me. About everything and nothing. Politics, world events, my favorite ice cream flavor, good books I'd read… Guys my age didn't do that, and for once, it was nice to be valued for something other than my body.

He woke up my mind, made me take notice, and my body had followed. My body was on *fire* for him now. For the past week, I hadn't been able to stop fantasizing about him. About what his mouth would taste like. If he'd be gentle or rough when he played with my breasts, sucked my nipples. If he'd groan or hum deep in his throat when he sank inside. If he'd be patient and play my body like an instrument, or if he'd be greedy and take only what he needed…

I let my eyelids fall closed, images from last night flashing in my mind. I could practically feel his breath across my breasts, the smooth, practiced thrusting of his fingers inside me. I could *definitely* still feel the way my pussy had been stretched—the tiny ache the only physical reminder I had that last night had actually happened.

But I had his words, too. He couldn't take those back, no matter how hard he tried. He could run away. He could avoid me. He could even ignore me, but he could never pluck those words out of existence and put them back in his mouth. *You have no idea how much I want to taste you, Genesis.* I shivered in remembrance of him using my full name. Like it had meaning. Like I wasn't just a faceless vessel with which to get off. *I want to bury my face in that sweet pussy and lap up every drop.*

Yeah. He could deny all he wanted, but I knew

the truth. And sooner or later, it was going to come out again, even if I had to rely on every weapon in my arsenal and put them all into play.

———

So much for my arsenal.

It'd been two weeks. Two fucking weeks since that night in the family room, and I hadn't seen Brandon once. Sure, he left me notes—incredibly impersonal notes—on the counter, made sure the fridge was full, even had some meals prepped and stocked in the freezer. He was *coddling* me like I was a child, and I hated it.

I wasn't his daughter, and it was time he stopped attempting to force that idea on himself. I knew it'd be difficult to get something like that out of his head, but I also knew he'd been able to push past it at some point. Otherwise, that night never would've happened.

I glanced at the clock. Two hours remained of my shift at Sin, and then I'd head back to Brandon's. I wasn't even sure why I was excited to get home tonight. It'd be the same thing it had been the past two weeks. If he happened to be home—which he rarely was—his door would be shut tight. It might as well have had a giant padlock on it, a huge sign proclaiming *stay the fuck away.*

I was going crazy in the house, so different from my own. Too big and too quiet and too hollow. But even though my mom was getting better, was growing stronger every day, she still wanted me staying with Brandon. She didn't have to spell out the reason she wanted me there, but I knew it was because she thought I'd be less lonely there while she was still in the hospital. Truth was, I felt lonelier while Brandon was in the next room than I did when I was entirely by myself.

But if she needed me to be there so she could focus on her rehab to get better, then that was what I'd do. I just hoped I didn't go crazy in the meantime.

The bell above the door jingled, and Harper, Sin's owner, called out, "Gen, can you get that?"

"On it," I said, pausing from stocking the new display with today's shipment. I'd seen more dildos than I could count, but I had to admit this one was a nice cock, modeled after a popular porn star. But then I thought of what I'd felt in Brandon's pajama pants, and I knew he'd put the eight inches of veined, silicone perfection to shame.

I forced thoughts of Brandon's cock out of my head and made my way to the front of the store, seeing a familiar head of almost-black hair. "Bailey, hey! Damn, girl, another one?" I asked with a laugh.

"Oh my God." She giggled, closing her eyes as a fierce blush climbed up her cheeks. "It's not normal, right? What kind of person goes through four vibrators in three months?"

"Um, the kind who isn't getting laid regularly?"

"I wish it were just that," she said.

Bartenders got a rep for being free therapists,

but here was the real truth: in a town as small as Temperance Falls, one that prided itself on the wholesome image it liked to portray, there was no one you could trust more than the person selling you your sex toys. Which was why I knew exactly what her problem was.

"Hot Doctor still got the nanny all worked up?"

Said nanny groaned in frustration. "So worked up, it's ridiculous. I've gone months before without getting any, and it never had this effect on me. It's living in that house. The sexual tension might as well be a blanket I wrap around myself as soon as I walk through the door."

I hummed in response, for the first time being able to empathize with every word that came out of her mouth. "I find myself in a similar situation."

"Really?" she asked, drawing out the word. Perking up, she leaned toward me. "Any tips?"

Snorting, I shook my head. "I wish. He pretends I'm not even there. And that's during the times he even bothers to come home when I'm not asleep."

"Ahh, avoidance." She nodded and tucked her hair behind her ear. "Sometimes I wish Josh would do that. Then maybe I wouldn't be blowing through all the vibrators on the island. But with his kid, it's kind of impossible."

"Believe me, avoidance isn't great." I might as well have been a stranger renting a room in Brandon's house for all the attention he'd been paying me.

"Okay, girls, it's time to stop dicking around, and starting *dicking around*, if you know what I mean." Harper came out of the back room, looking like a forties pinup star, and placed two bags on the counter, the shiny red of the lips of the logo vibrant against the stark black background. "You," she said, pointing to Bailey, "are going to be able to power the whole goddamn island pretty soon with the amount of sexual energy you have building up. I mean, hot doctor and the nanny? You're a porn script waiting to happen. And you"—she turned her gaze on me, her eyes narrowing—"don't think I haven't noticed how you've been these past two weeks. Honestly, girls, haven't you learned anything from me? If the men won't come to you, you go to *them*. And then you make them beg." She smiled—though it looked a little evil, to be perfectly honest—as she pushed the bags toward us.

"What's this?" I asked, my curiosity getting the better of me as I went over to peek. I moved aside the red tissue paper hiding the contents and got my first look at the vibrator inside—a brand-new model with ten different vibrating functions that I'd been waiting patiently to arrive. Glancing back at her, I raised my eyebrows in question.

The only answer was a smirk and wink tossed in our direction, before she turned around and headed toward the back room again. Over her shoulder, she said, "Make sure to do a thorough analysis of it, Gen. Hands-on experience to share with the customers and all that. And get out of here. What better time to try it out than when he thinks you aren't due back home for another couple hours?"

Bailey and I watched her sashay through the red velvet curtain into the space separating the shop from the storage room and her office, our gaping mouths mirroring each other.

With a raised eyebrow in Bailey's direction, I went around to the back of the cash wrap, grabbed my purse, then reached up and looped the bag's handles over my hand. Shrugging, I said, "Can't hurt, right?"

Maybe Harper was on to something. Brandon knew my schedule, knew when I'd be home and when I'd be otherwise occupied. Hell, I'd even fallen into a routine of going to see my mom—the same time every day. He knew when it'd be safe for him to be home, and when he needed to make himself scarce.

Looked like it was time to shake things up again. I had some begging to listen to.

chapter five

BRANDON

THIRTEEN DAYS OF nothing but work, whiskey, and jacking off left me feeling as if I could explode at any moment. I'd been snapping at my assistants, running my team into the ground every day, and avoiding my own home like the plague. What the fuck was wrong with me?

Oh, that's right. I wanted to go balls deep until I had a woman the same age as my daughter screaming my name. That was what. Those fucking red panties just kept haunting me.

I adjusted myself through my pants for the hundredth time that day and took a deep breath. The McIntyre Steel folder—red, of course—sat open on my desk, the documents still unread. Clark had scheduled a meeting to touch base on the progress, but I couldn't concentrate. Too many thoughts of red hair, black tank tops, and all the glory of what was underneath consumed my brain. The guilt wasn't helping, either.

I'd avoided Gen since the night I'd accosted her on my couch, communicating in nothing but Post-it notes. Callous? Yes. Better for her? I could only hope. But at what cost? She had to think I was the biggest asshole alive, though she hadn't yet left. Whether that was because of her mom or me, I had no idea. I sort of hoped it was the latter. Sort of dreaded it, too.

"Brandon, old boy. I haven't seen you in weeks." Clark strolled into my office without knocking on the closed door, a habit that had always rubbed me the wrong way. If I dared to do the same, he'd chew me up and spit me out for disrespecting him.

I rose from my seat, thankful for the sport coat I'd kept on as it would hide the erection I couldn't seem to lose. Even when Gen wasn't with me, she was on my mind. Everything red reminded me of her; everything black stole my attention. I needed to focus.

"Clark. So good to see you," I said, forcing my lips into a smile. "I never got to say thank you for coming to Evie's graduation party. It was good to see you and Brock."

"Yes, yes. Great party, though your daughter certainly pulled a number on Brock." He frowned as he took a seat, eyeing me hard. "He's been heartbroken."

I had to work to unclench my jaw. Clark was the biggest name in real estate and development in the Midwest. He'd also been my boss and mentor since I was a fresh-faced kid with nothing more than a bachelor's degree and a toddler on my hip. He taught me everything I knew about business, but he also expected a lot in return. We had current deals in process in six countries and on three continents, not to mention just about every state in the union. Business hours? That meant all day, every day including weekends—for me and my team, not so much for him.

As business partners, we should have been on an even playing field, but Clark had made sure I could only buy forty-five percent of the business when the opportunity had come up. He held fifty-one to be majority stockholder. Brock held the other four. I was outnumbered, therefore, always at risk. And the bastard never let me forget it.

"Evie tried to be kind," I said, sitting back and forcing my shoulders to relax. "But she wanted to choose a different path."

"Yes, I saw her and her new path yesterday at the diner. Interesting pairing, your daughter and your best friend."

"Yes, well…" No words would come. As much as I wanted to defend my daughter, defend Nate for choosing her, I couldn't. I struggled accepting their relationship because she was so much younger than he was, yet there I went, chasing after a girl the same age as Evie. I was just as bad, just as wrong, but it felt just as right as what Nate had told me about how he fell for Evie. What the fuck was I supposed to say?

Clark scowled at my non-answer. "I would hope

this sort of thing doesn't run in the family. I'd hate to have to exert my control over the board should any infidelities come to light."

"I'm not married," I said, taking a deep breath before continuing. "And my personal life is completely above board. Always has been. You have nothing to worry about."

"Good, good. Now that this ugliness is out of the way, let's get to why I'm here. When are we closing the McIntyre Steel property?"

I grabbed the paperwork and let my mouth run on autopilot, trying like hell to ignore the yearning in my gut for the girl at home. The one I felt more connected to than I'd thought possible. The one I was trying to stay away from.

The one who could destroy my entire life if I surrendered to temptation again.

I trudged my way through the front door long before the sun went down. Odd time for me to be home, but I knew Gen would be working. That left me with the house to myself. I had plenty of time to seek out every sign of her having been there, jack off, grab a quick bite, and be back at my office before her workday was even over.

First stop, the whiskey bottle in my office. I loosened my tie and undid the top button of my shirt, giving myself room to breathe. Second stop, the couch in the family room. I was a sick fucker for getting so worked up about a piece of furniture, but I couldn't help myself. I loved imagining her there, remembering her all wide-eyed and flushed. Wishing she was there again. She'd sprawl out, her red hair falling like flames to the floor, her legs opening in invitation. I'd crawl between her thighs, lift her wet pussy to my mouth, and I'd get to taste her. Finally. It was all I wanted to do—lick that sweet pussy until she came on my tongue. Drink down every ounce of her pleasure. I hadn't gone down on a woman in almost twenty years, hadn't even considered it before Gen. Now, it was all I could think about. All I wanted. A craving that wouldn't let me go.

Every day, I followed the same routine. I'd drink whiskey and imagine how ripe Gen would taste. How sweet and wet she would be. When the need got to be too much, when my cock was hard and my head filled with pictures of her red hair and pale skin, I'd rush upstairs to my shower so I could stroke myself in peace. The whole time I would run my hand over my cock, tugging from base to tip, I'd pretend Gen was in the house with me, living with me not because she had to but because she wanted to. Because she was mine. And later, after I'd come at least twice, I'd head back to work pretending she had never been in my house at all just to get through the rest of the day. That was my hell.

Just like every other day for the past two weeks, I grabbed my whiskey, sat down on the couch, and let my imagination run wild. But my plans for solitary stimulation exploded when—as I sat with one hand holding a glass of whiskey and the other rubbing my cock over my pants—I heard a tsking sound from the hallway.

"Is that the kind of thing you normally do when I'm not here, Brandon?"

If I'd been half the man I should have been, I'd have been embarrassed about being caught jacking off. I'd have gotten up off the couch and headed back to the office. I wouldn't have even offered Gen more than a casual apology as I blew past her.

But I wasn't that good of a man, especially not after two weeks of needing her, wanting her, knowing she was sleeping two doors down from me and not being able to take her. Not even close.

I gave myself one final stroke, eyeing the tight-as-fuck jeans and tank top she wore with more than a little interest before dropping my hand to my thigh and taking another sip.

"Shouldn't you be at work?" I asked, my eyes refusing to leave the soft curves of her body.

"I am working."

"In that?" I set my whiskey down on the end table and gestured to the tank top barely covering her tits. Fuck, I wanted to rip it off her. Wanted to yank it over her head and taste all that sweet flesh.

"Fits the part," Gen said with a simple shrug. "My boss wants me to try out this new vibrator and report back."

It took a few seconds for her words to register. Something about my sweet Gen and vibrator didn't go together at first, but then they did. I sat straight up, stumbling over words until I finally yelled, "You brought a sex toy home with you?"

Just the thought, the image of her with her fingers between her legs, her nipples tight as she brought herself closer to the edge. Just the possibility that she might have been thinking of me when she did that... I had no words. Not really. Maybe a handful, though they weren't at all what I really wanted to focus on. "Where the hell do you work?"

She didn't flinch, didn't even react to my raised voice with anything more than a quirked eyebrow. "Sin."

"Fuck," I breathed, the sound long and drawn-out even to my own ears. Fucking hell, she was going to kill me. I closed my eyes, fighting back the need to touch her. To drag her ass under mine and fuck the ever-loving shit out of her. She worked at the sex shop across town? How had I not known that? Half the guys on the island had probably hit on her at one point or another as they trekked inside the two-story brick building for their porn and sexual accoutrements. I knew that shop, had been the one to sell it to the current owner's grandmother too many years ago to think about. I'd been in every room, every floor, in every closet and niche. And now I could picture Gen in there, her hair loose, her jeans and tanks so much sexier than all the lingerie in the place.

And all the men who'd be trying, looking to get a date, a touch, a taste. Fuck and no.

"You can't work there."

Gen laughed, as if what I was saying was a joke.

"I hate to tell you this, Brandon, but I can work wherever I want."

She moved across the floor, a lioness on the hunt, coming closer with every step. Rolling her hips in a way that should have been illegal. Fuck, I liked being her prey. Too much. Way too much.

"Gen, for my sanity, you can't work there. I can't get arrested for beating the shit out of someone at the local smut shack."

More steps. A sexy sway to her hips that made my mouth water as she moved closer. "Why would you beat the shit out of anyone?"

And wasn't that the question of the hour? I'd given her a piece of me, taken something from her, then walked away and pretended she didn't exist. And for what? To lose my mind every day thinking about her? To push her away to save myself some possible professional embarrassment? I was an idiot. She deserved better than that, better than me. She deserved to be loved and cared for, to be spoiled. To be worshiped every single day.

And I planned on doing that, starting right then.

"You don't know?" I grabbed a belt loop of her jeans as soon as she was close enough, yanking her until her knees bumped the edge of the couch. Needing to have my hands on her, but not convinced I should. Not sure if she'd accept my touch. "You don't get it?"

"What I get is that you liked what we did right here on this couch, but then you ran like a coward. And now you want to tell me what to do?" She placed one knee on the couch, brushing mine, spreading her legs just enough to force my eyes to her covered pussy. The jeans were so much sexier than the tiny shorts she'd worn the other night. Left more to my imagination, and my imagination was good. Strong. Especially in regards to Gen. Unable to stop myself, I ran my hand up her thigh, stroking my fingers over the seam covering her pussy. Teasing her, giving her the chance to pull away. She didn't. In fact, she rocked closer. Oh yeah, I was closing this deal.

"You know what I think?" I tugged her forward, forcing her to straddle my lap. The move was so much like two weeks before, my cock twitched at the thought of a repeat. "I think deep down, you want me to tell you what to do. You want me to care enough to say no."

"Nope. Here's the thing—I'm not one of your subordinates, Mr. Catalpa. What I want is for you to man up and admit you like me. That we have chemistry. Or is that too much to ask?"

Oh hell. Her calling me by my surname should not have turned me on so much, but it did. As did the way her eyes practically glittered as she looked me over, a predator and her prey. But if she thought I was simply surrendering, she was wrong. I still had a little power here, and I was going to use it.

"Everything about you is too much, Genesis." I flipped us both, dropping her to lie on the couch and sliding down her body until my chest rested between her spread legs, my knees on the ground. Lower still, tugging the denim down and biting a path over her hip. Breathing in the deep, delicious scent of her need. "You know what I wanted to do to you that night?"

"Fuck me?"

"Yes, but that wasn't all." I unfastened her jeans, kissing the flesh revealed. But as I slid them down over her hips, I froze. Motherfucking red—lace and tight and skimpy as fuck. I could already tell. I'd dreamed of those exact panties for weeks, and she was wearing them? I was going to see her ass cupped by the red lace of my fantasies? I was done for. "Fuck me, I love these panties."

Gen chuckled, her body shaking against mine. "Focus, Brandon. What else did you want to do?"

Everything, I wanted to answer. But I couldn't— not yet. Not until I had her ready for me. Once I admitted my need, there'd be no holding back. I pulled Gen's jeans lower still, spreading her thighs as soon as the fabric cleared her knees. With one hand on her hip, fingers stroking the lace there, I took the time to remove the denim from around her ankles before gifting myself with a look at her in the panties that had haunted my dreams. Before taking a deep breath and seeing how good my imagination really was. How accurate. When I had her legs free, I kissed her knee and turned my head enough to look. To see. To finally take in the vision of her in lace.

One look, and every ounce of blood I had rushed south to my already rock-hard cock. That slip of red fabric covering her pussy was wet—soaked, really. Her desire a physical thing I got to see, to touch, to taste. Pulled tight across her, the fabric fit snug and low in a way that seemed almost obscene. Accentuating her curves even as she sprawled across the couch. Bright red against pale white. Pure perfection on the seduction scale.

"Brandon," Gen said, her voice breathy. "Tell me."

Her hands were in my hair, pulling. I groaned and bit her thigh, just a nip, really. Just enough to tempt myself with her flavor.

"I wanted to taste you. I wanted to lick this pussy until you came, screaming my name." I teased a knuckle over the fabric covering her, desperate to touch, to make sure the red wasn't a dream. She shivered, so I did it again, inching closer, forcing her knees apart with my shoulders. "I still want to."

Gen didn't hesitate. Didn't falter for a second. She looked me square in the eye the second I tore my gaze away from those dream panties, her face flushed and a challenge obvious. "So, do it."

With a smirk I couldn't have wiped away if I tried, I leaned in and opened my mouth on that seductive red fabric. I ran my teeth over her, carefully biting down to catch just the fabric, even as I purposely rubbed against her clit, and then I pulled back. The red lace came with me, trailing down her legs, baring her to me in a slow slide that made my cock leak with precome. When the fabric hit her knees, I let go of it and used my hand instead, shoving the scrap of fabric into my pocket before moving up her thighs once more.

"Those are mine now." I bit down on her thigh again, a little harder this time, making her jump.

"You're taking my favorite panties?"

"I've jacked off to thoughts of you wearing those too many times to count." I spread her wider, pulling her ass right to the edge of the couch so I could have access to all of her. Every sweet, pink inch on display for me. "I think I earned them."

"You don't earn them by getting yourself off. You earn them by getting me off. Think you can do it?"

"Is that a challenge?" I licked a path along the side of her pussy, barely letting my tongue tease where I knew she wanted it. She was so soft and hot, so motherfucking tempting. I was going to enjoy every single second of this. "Because I accept."

I gave her one small kiss before spreading her with my thumbs so I could lick her clit. Gen jerked and moaned, her hands falling to my shoulders before returning to my hair as I flicked and sucked and teased. When I knew I had her good and ready, when my chin was wet from rubbing against where she was swollen with need, I dragged two fingers along the seam of her thigh and slid them inside her.

"Holy shit," I groaned as I tore my mouth from her clit, pumping my fingers deeper with every press and pull. "How is this pussy so fucking hot? Are you burning up inside, baby? You need me to own this sweet pussy and make you come?"

Gen arched and shuddered, tightening around my fingers. "Holy shit, yes."

"I shouldn't fucking want you, but I do." I closed my eyes, resting my forehead against her thigh. Concentrating on every breath from Gen, every shiver, every clench as I worked her pussy with my hand. "How the fuck am I supposed to resist you?"

"I never said you had to."

I wanted to believe her, to give in and be sure us being together wouldn't blow up in my face at some point. Doubt lingered, though. Worry about her age, about my job, about how the people of Temperance Falls would react to us together. But when Gen arched her back and dropped her knees, rocked her hips and rode my fucking hand, I was done. I couldn't imagine giving her up, couldn't stop what I was doing, couldn't resist the chance to taste her as she came. She was so wet, so tight and perfect. So fucking responsive as I teased. I had to have her. And once I had her, she'd be mine. Forever.

Unable to resist her taste, I brought my mouth back to her clit, licking and sucking as I kept my hand moving. As I focused on giving her everything I could, on making sure she came at my hands. That I gave her the pleasure she needed. Ignoring my own wants and needs, I spent every second working her pussy. Owning it. Worshiping her sex until she was a writhing, sweating, moaning mess of a girl ready to explode. And then I curled my fingers and pushed her right over the edge.

Gen came with a yelp and a groan that had my cock leaking. Back arched, legs hugging my shoulders, she rocked and shook as she milked my fingers. As she tugged at my hair and chanted my name. I kept up the assault on her clit, kept licking just enough to push her through, even though I wanted nothing more than to pull out my cock and yank her down on top of me.

Apparently, Gen had the same idea.

Without warning, she practically lunged off the couch, knocking me backward and straddling my hips as I pulled my hand from between us. Her mouth found mine, her arms wrapping around my neck, but that was the end of her leading. I gripped her hips and yanked her closer to settle her weight over my cock, kissing her deeply.

"You taste like me," she whispered before groaning and diving in for another kiss. And fuck me, that might have been the hottest thing a woman had ever said to me. I couldn't hold back another moment.

I had my pants open in a matter of seconds, my cock in hand right after. Before I even broke the kiss, I was sliding inside the heaven of Gen's pussy. So hot, so wet, so fucking soft. And so bare.

"Tell me you're on birth control," I said, pulling her down, dropping my head to her shoulder as I drove in deep. I didn't want to fuck up her future, but I couldn't stop. Couldn't pull myself away. I needed to know before we did something that couldn't be taken back.

Gen nodded, gasping as I thrust harder. "Yeah. The pill."

"Thank fuck for that." I sucked her bottom lip into my mouth as I thrust upward over and over again. This was what I'd been dying for. Beyond her taste, beyond knowing how my fingers felt wrapped up inside her, this was the ultimate goal. My cock deep in her pussy, her body wrapped around mine. Both of us hot and sweaty and breathing way too hard as we satisfied the cravings within us. As we fucked the need and desire right out of each other.

Needing more leverage, I tossed her back and followed her down, bringing her knees to my chest to keep her legs open even as her pussy tightened around me. Fuck, so good. So tight. There was no way I was going to last. One hand between us so I could thrum her clit with my thumb, the other holding one of her wrists above her head, I fucked her like a man possessed. Like a man who'd finally gotten everything he'd ever wanted in one sexy little package. Like she deserved to be fucked.

And when she came, when she screamed my name and arched her back to press her hips into mine, I followed. Knowing this was it. She was it. I'd give up everything for her, for more moments like this one. There would be no walking away this time.

This was everything.

chapter six

GENESIS

WHEN WAS THE last time I'd been this sated? When I'd been able to feel the bliss washing over me, from my head to my toes and settling into every crevice in between? When I'd gotten fucked within an inch of my life?

Never, that was when.

Even my prized vibrator, to whom I'd sworn my eternal love and devotion, didn't hold a candle to Brandon and his magnificent cock or his glorious tongue.

And, sweet Jesus, that tongue.

I groaned, threading my fingers through his hair as he went down on me. Again. It was almost dawn, and I was exhausted from the workout he'd put me through in the past ten hours. I was deliciously sore in all the right places, but I didn't want him to stop.

Even after too many orgasms to count, I wanted more. I wanted whatever he'd give me. So when he woke me up with his tongue stroking my clit? I spread my legs wider and graciously took what he offered.

"God, you're good at that," I said, panting. "How do you already know—*ohh.*"

He gave another swirl of his tongue around my clit, then pulled back as he slowed his pumping fingers. "I've been jacking my cock to thoughts of all the things I wanted to do to you for weeks now. It's about time I got to put them to use on this pussy."

Fuck. This man and his filthy mouth. I'd never been one for dirty talk before. Probably because the guys I'd been with had thought a running porn script would turn me on. But, Brandon? The way he almost couldn't control what he was saying? Like if he'd been in the right frame of mind, he never would've let those thoughts tumble from his lips? It was divine. It was like he was voicing every dirty thought he'd ever had about me, and that made me feel…wanted. It made me feel like this wasn't just a single fuck—or a single night of fucking, anyway—for him.

He sped up his movements, his tongue working me with no end in sight, and I was a goner. "Oh shit, I'm gonna—"

"C'mon, baby. Give it to me. I want to feel it."

As I moaned my head off, he stroked me through my orgasm, lazily swiping his tongue all over my pussy, making my hips jump off the bed when he grazed my clit. When the last pulse washed over me, I used all the strength I could muster and clutched his hair in my fingers, pulling him up the length of my body until his face was level with mine.

"This is a little early for a wake-up call, don't you think?" I asked as he settled his weight on me, his hard cock sliding against my pussy.

"It's never too early for my favorite meal."

He cut off my sleep-roughened laugh with his mouth, his tongue snaking between my lips to tangle with mine. Groaning, I wrapped my arms around his shoulders, loving how the muscles bunched and flexed under my roaming hands. My nipples brushed against soft hair dusting his chest, tightening even further. Even the way this man kissed me shot every past experience I'd ever had out of the water. He didn't just focus on my mouth—oh no. He nipped at my chin, licked along the shell of my ear, sank his teeth into the curve where my shoulder met my neck. I never knew where he was going next, so all I could do was lie there and breathe. Okay, pant. I was panting, but I couldn't help it. Brandon had me halfway to another orgasm just from his kisses.

Knowing if I didn't take control right then, he'd take those kisses and trail them down my body until he was tongue-deep in my pussy again, I pushed against his shoulders and rolled us over. Sitting astride his hips, I slid along the hard length of him, making sure the head of his cock bumped my clit with every pass. I could've sat there all day, rubbing myself against him and getting off again and again, but I had work to do.

With a kiss to his jaw, I started my trek down

his body, stopping at my newly discovered favorite locations. The bite of my teeth on his broad shoulder, a brush of my lips along his collarbone, the flick of my tongue against a pebbled nipple. Honestly, my fantasizing hadn't done him justice. He was perfection with his model good looks and his chiseled body. This man should've been carved in stone and had a statue erected in the center of town with a plaque that read, *God of Cunnilingus and Orgasms.*

He groaned and lifted his hips, thrusting his cock against me as he did. "Where are you going?"

Resting my chin on his sternum, I rotated my hips and grinned. "To return the favor."

Rather than let me go along my merry little way, he stilled me with unyielding hands at my hips, settling me firmly over his cock. "Not now. I want to watch you. I want to see your face when you come," he said as he thrust up with his hips.

How he managed to regain control even in a submissive position was beyond me, but there was no denying he held every ounce as my head fell forward on a groan. Lifting my head from his chest, I leaned over him so our lips just brushed. "I think you're the only guy on earth who doesn't like to have his dick sucked."

He nipped my lip, sucking my bottom one into his mouth and releasing it with a pop. "I never said I didn't like it, but I want to watch you. I haven't been able to watch in so long." Holding me in place with a firm hand on my hip, he guided me to take him inside my body, both of us groaning as I sank down until he filled me completely.

I breathed out a sigh as my eyes fluttered closed, loving the exquisite ache he created in me every time he was inside. While I hadn't exactly banged my way across the island, I was far from a virgin, but it'd never been like this for me before. It was like my body had been asleep before Brandon came along, and then he lit me up like a firecracker.

Again and again, I rolled my hips, taking him deep and letting him retreat, until the languid pace wasn't enough for me anymore. Pushing back, I sat up, both of us groaning at how deep he went. With a swivel of my hips, I looked down to find him staring up at me, almost…reverently. His eyes were full of heat and lust, yes, but there was something else there, too. Something I was both scared and exhilarated at the prospect of.

"Is it always like this for you?" I whispered. Not wanting to know. *Desperate* to know.

"Never. It's never been…" He closed his eyes, a sharp shake of his head before he looked up at me again. "You're the only one, Genesis. The only person who's ever gotten this close. You've become my greatest need."

Holy shit. Who *was* this man? It was like he'd been sent here to fulfill every single one of my needs—and some I didn't even realize I had.

And he'd somehow made me speechless, so instead of responding with words, I let my body speak for me as I rocked against him. As I kissed him and caressed him and took him as deep inside me as he could get.

Eventually, we got lost in our bodies, the ache

taking over once the soft swivel of my hips wasn't enough to get us there. With hands framed wide on my hips, one thumb pressing against my clit, Brandon held me above him and thrust into me from below. The sound of our bodies slapping together mixing with our harsh breaths were the only noises in the otherwise quiet house.

After the slow buildup, I didn't stand a chance. Not when he was working my body so well. Not when he was looking up at me like I was everything he'd ever wanted. My orgasm swept over me, the rolling waves crashing through my body. And even though I was nearly lost to the feelings he'd evoked inside me, I wasn't so far gone as to miss the way he thrust deep as he pulled me down onto him, repeating my name over and over like a prayer as he spilled inside me.

The boneless form of my body collapsed against his chest, our rapid breaths matching one another. Brandon's soft puffs of air settled against the top of my head, and though I knew it wasn't possible with real life creeping in, I wanted nothing more than to stay here. Lie in bed all day and do nothing but talk and laugh and map each other's bodies with our tongues.

"Any time you want to wake me up with your tongue on my clit, I'm totally fine with that, FYI," I mumbled into his chest.

Brandon chuckled and trailed his fingers in a soft caress down my back. "You'll have to get used to early mornings, then. I'm already late for work."

I turned my head to glance at the clock on his

nightstand, seeing the glowing numbers proclaiming it was o'dark thirty. "It's not even six in the morning. How can you be late already?"

"I've got clients in time zones where they're eating lunch by now. Someone needs to be there to make sure they're taken care of."

This man, always taking care of everyone else. Evie, for the past eighteen years. Me, since I'd temporarily moved in. All his clients he worked with eighty hours a week. But it wasn't everyone else I was worried about. It was him. If he wasn't careful, he'd work himself into an early grave. Or a late grave with nothing to show for his life but loneliness. I didn't want that for him.

I didn't want that for *us*. If there even was an us…

"Who takes care of you, Brandon?"

He hummed, the sound vibrating against my cheek as it rested against his chest. His kiss was soft but lasting, the feel of it tingling long after he pulled away. "Just me. Why? Are you offering?"

I tipped my head back to look into his eyes, trying to get a read on his sincerity. The tone of his voice, the softness of his eyes, the light caresses of his fingers…everything told me he was honestly asking me the question. And I felt like everything we had hung in the balance based on my answer.

The thing was, I *did* want to be the one who took care of him. What we had between us was fast and it was unconventional, but I couldn't deny the chemistry we had in spades. And the thing I loved the most was that it wasn't just sexual chemistry between us. We could talk for hours—*had* talked for hours—about everything and nothing, and not get bored.

But even knowing all that, there was one thing I couldn't get out of my mind…

"What about Evie?"

Every one of his muscles tightened up under me, the soft brushes of his fingers freezing along my back for a split second. Then it was like it hadn't happened.

"Evie has Nate," he said as he rolled us to our sides so we were facing each other. He pressed a too-brief kiss to my lips. "I put my life on hold for her. I gave up on the possibility of finding someone just for me to make sure she was happy and had everything she could want, but that part of my life is over now. She's my daughter, and she'll always have a place here. But it's my turn to live. My turn to get what I want."

"This is going to come as a shock to her. I've never—I mean, I haven't mentioned…" I took a deep breath and exhaled, needing to just say it, even if it made me sound like a starry-eyed teenager with a short-term crush. Despite knowing I wasn't, that what I was feeling for him went beyond a mere crush—went beyond anything I'd felt before—I was still nervous to tell him. "This"—I gestured between us—"is sorta new for me. Before her graduation party, I'd never…"

"Never mentioned you thought I was a DILF?"

"*Oh my God!*" I buried my face into his shoulder, certain I was at least the shade of an apple. "You heard that?"

"No." He pulled back enough so he could get a

hand between us, and with a firm finger under my chin, forced me to look up at him. Even in the dimness of the bedroom, I could see the laugh lines crinkling around his eyes from how hard he was smiling. "Do you really think I'm a DILF?"

"Um, hello? Have you looked in a mirror lately?" I asked, gesturing to his fuckhot body sprawled out next to me, the V of his hips peeking out from above the sheet and pointing to my new favorite toy.

Taking advantage of my attention being otherwise occupied, he pounced, rolling us until he was over me, his hips settled between my parted thighs. "I'd rather look at you. Naked. Every single day."

Even though it'd been fun and laughs just moments ago, there was that sincerity back in his voice again, and I'd have to have been blind to miss the emotion in his eyes. "Every day?"

With a single, decisive nod, he said, "I told you. It's my turn to get what I want, and I want you. Here. With me."

I lifted my head so our lips brushed together with every word. "I want to be here with you, too."

He stared at me for a moment as we shared breath, and then with a groan, he kissed me. The once-again hard length of him slid along my pussy, teasing my clit enough to get me panting, and then with a gentle push of his hips, he was buried inside me.

"Again?" I breathed, fingernails scraping down his back as I wrapped my legs around him to take him deeper.

"Want more." He pressed his face into my neck,

his lips covering every square inch as he kissed and licked and sucked. "Want so much more."

All I could do was arch into him, taking whatever he was giving, because I wanted every bit of the *more* he was offering.

chapter seven

BRANDON

I HAD NEVER hated my job more than I did the moment Clark walked into my office the following Thursday night. What was supposed to be date night for Genesis and me.

This wouldn't be good.

"Brandon, my boy. How are things?"

I stood, fighting the urge to scowl at the man. I'd been planning to leave, having not been home to have dinner with my girl in days. I'd promised her I wouldn't be late tonight. I had even made a reservation at the best restaurant on the island so we could spend some serious time together without being naked. We'd be run through the gossip mills by morning, but I didn't care. I wanted to show her off, to take her someplace nice, to spoil her a little.

I had a feeling I was about to break my promise.

"Things are well, Clark." I shook his hand, darting a glance over his shoulder as my assistant snuck toward the front door. I couldn't blame her. "What can I do for you so late?"

"Late? Since when is seven late? I thought you were a full-timer."

I choked back my automatic—and highly unprofessional—response and tried to smile at his boisterous laugh, but I couldn't. The only thing on my mind, the only thought in my head, was Genesis sitting at home waiting for me. Probably all dressed up. Excited, even. I was an asshole.

"Yes, well." I took a deep breath, refocusing. "It's been a long week." Too long, in fact. I'd spent too much time away from home. Something I'd rarely thought about while it was happening. Sure, there had been times when I'd missed events for Evie over the years, but I'd been busy trying to make sure she had everything she could want. Everything she could need. The best life I could give her.

But with Genesis, things were different. I hated my long hours, hated knowing she was alone and probably lonely without me. Evie craved her solitude—she loved the quiet house, needed time alone to recharge herself. Genesis—well, she wasn't Evie. She sought out people to interact with, and her vibrant personality drew them to her. She was like the first bit of sun after a cold winter, warming everyone, making people smile along with her. And I had been soaking her in this past week. Instead of jumping up in the morning to get to work, wanting to close every deal as quickly as I could, I lingered in bed with her. I lost my concentration during the day and found myself daydreaming about her. I spent hours wanting to be around Genesis instead of my team, needing to feel her touch. Her warmth. And she needed my attention as well.

After almost twenty years of my nose to the grindstone for Clark, it was time for me to focus on things outside of Wilkinson Properties.

"I hope whatever you need can be dealt with tomorrow. I was just about to head home for a late dinner."

Clark wasn't as good at hiding his scowl as I was. "I assumed you'd be working on the McIntyre deal."

"I have been. We're a hairbreadth from closing. Just need the final results from the water test and a few signatures. I'll have it finished next week."

"Don't slack on me now, Brandon. We've still got a lot of deals to work through. Deals that will bring us all a lot of money."

Money. Always the fucking money. "Yes, of course."

"Good." He grinned in a way that seemed utterly predatory. "So I'll see those finalized McIntyre papers on my desk Monday morning, then?"

Bastard. "Sure," I choked out, my anger hot under my skin. "Yes. No problem."

But it was a problem, and as Clark left the office—probably heading home for the night—my guilt at leaving Genesis alone so much only multiplied. I wanted to spend time with her, to talk to her. I wanted to get to know her as a person and give her a chance to get to know me. We'd spent our mornings and nights naked, our needs insatiable, but I wanted more than a physical relationship with her. I wanted every part of her.

But my job stood in the way.

Just as I was sitting down to look over the McIntyre documents for the thousandth time, my phone rang. Genesis, of course.

"Hey, baby."

"Hey," she said, her voice happy. Fuck. "We're going to be late for our reservations at Nonno Pino's if you don't hurry home. Or did you need to meet me there?"

I sighed, staring at the red folder on my desk. My shoulders were stiff with the stress of trying to balance my desire to go home and my need to accomplish my work. I could only hope she'd understand. "I've got bad news."

"Brandon. Are you serious?"

"I know, and I'm sorry. It's this McIntyre deal."

"It's always a deal, isn't it? You forget I've been around for a long time. I've heard all about your deals over the years—how they made you miss this and that. It's a goddamn miracle you made it to Evie's graduation party."

I closed my eyes, trying hard not to feel like both the worst father and lover on the planet. Trying and failing. "I'm sorry."

Her laugh held no humor, no light. She was mad. "Getting really damn sick of hearing that. It's been less than a week, and this is the fourth time you've canceled on me because of some shit at work. Usually, when people say they're sorry, they try to make amends for it and actually *change*."

I closed my eyes, rubbing my forehead with my free hand. Staring out the window at the night sky over the water. "It's just an hour or so. Let me get through with this contract review, and I'll be home. I can…I don't know. Maybe I can cook for us." Shit. I'd probably need to stop at the grocery store.

But Genesis didn't seem impressed by my offer. She took a deep breath, the static of her exhale making me wince. "Don't worry about it. I'll be fine on my own."

And then she was gone.

I must have stared at that dark screen for ten minutes, must have mulled over my wants versus my needs versus my responsibilities even longer. In the end, only one could win.

I'd spent almost twenty years giving everything I could to Wilkinson Properties. I'd climbed through every hoop, made the Wilkinson family more money than any person could possibly need in a lifetime. I had sacrificed everything for them.

They could survive one night without me closing a deal.

I grabbed the McIntyre Steel folder and shoved it into my briefcase before digging out my keys. I may have fucked up date night, but there had to be a way to rescue it. Had to be a way to make things up to my beautiful girl.

There had to be a way to make her smile.

GENESIS

———

Being a friend of Evie's for as long as I'd been, I was no stranger to Brandon's excuses. No stranger to the empty house or the *so sorry I can't make it* calls.

I'd just never before been such a front row participant.

Too pissed to stay in the dress I made a special trip to the apartment to grab for tonight, I stripped it from my body, changing instead to boy shorts and an oversized sweatshirt. I swept back my freshly done hair, piling the mass on top of my head before scrubbing my face free of makeup. Then I trekked downstairs, raided the freezer for the emergency ice cream stash Evie kept there, and resigned myself to spending the night with a pint of Chunky Monkey and season six of *Gilmore Girls*.

That was where Brandon found me one and a half episodes later, the empty ice cream carton discarded on the end table. He stood at the edge of the family room, as if he was waiting for me to welcome him inside. He'd be waiting a long damn time because I refused to even *look* at him. I knew if I did, I'd forgive him. Like usual.

It'd only been a week, but he'd canceled on me more than he'd shown up. I didn't know what was going on between us, but from the way he talked, how he looked at me, it *felt* like we were something more than just a fling. And if that was the case, he needed to learn really damn early that I wasn't going to take the back seat—not to a job.

"Gen."

I ignored him, knowing full well how childish of me it was to do so. Didn't matter. I'd been looking forward to this night out…I *needed* it. Earlier in the day, I'd gotten the report that my mom was doing so well in her rehab they thought she'd be able to be released early.

What had originated as a celebratory meal stemming from news of my mom had quickly morphed into something different…something more. Brandon had made reservations at the nicest restaurant on the island instead of taking me to the diner like I'd anticipated. Maybe I'd read too much into it, thinking it'd been him taking a sort of public stance on us.

Turned out it didn't matter how much I read into it. Instead of going out—to celebrate my mom's imminent release, or whatever was between Brandon and me, or both—he'd left me alone. Again.

Interrupting my thoughts, he heaved a sigh and stepped into the family room, the rustling of paper and plastic moving along with him. And then he stood in front of me, several bags dangling from his fingertips, the unmistakable scents of Chinese wafting up from them. His dress shirt was untucked, tie loose around his neck, top two buttons undone. Looking hot as sin. I didn't know if it was the scent of the food or him that made my mouth water.

Willing myself not to get sucked into him like I always did, I said, "Do you mind?" Making a shooing motion with my hand, I looked around him, pretending my focus was on the TV and not the DILF in front of me.

"Genesis."

It took everything in me not to respond to his use of my full name, but I persevered. After a couple silent moments, he blew out a breath and stepped to the side. Instead of walking away like I thought he would, he began unloading the bags, right there on his fancy wood coffee table. By the time he was done, ten different containers sat opened, the aromas of kung pao chicken and chow mein overwhelming me. There was way too much for us to possibly eat, even if it was our first meal in three days.

Once everything was laid out, he took a seat on the coffee table, directly in my line of vision. He leaned toward me, elbows braced on his spread knees and hands clasped between them. "I'm an asshole— an overworked, overscheduled asshole. I know that. You know that." He reached out, cuffing his hand around my bare ankle, his thumb brushing against my skin. "I'm sorry. I'm so used to focusing solely on my work that I didn't weigh your emotions as highly as I should have. It was a mistake."

I could admit I hadn't had much experience with this kind of thing. Being in a relationship—was that what we were doing?—was something altogether new to me, and therefore, apologies from my partner were something I hadn't really had to deal with. But his seemed sincere. Seemed like it was more than just words.

After a few more seconds of silence, he said, "Baby…talk to me. Please." His voice was low, imploring, and regret and worry flashed plainly across his face.

It was the regret that got me.

"This is a waste." I gestured to the spread on the table. "We can't eat this much food."

He smiled, though it didn't quite reach his eyes. "I wasn't sure what you liked. You told Evie once that egg drop soup was disgusting, but that was all I could remember."

"It *is* disgusting. It looks like someone came in a pot of chicken broth." I scrunched up my nose. "If I wanted jizz in my mouth, I'd go to the source."

"I'll look forward to it." A small, sheepish grin curved up the corners of his mouth.

I hummed, raising an eyebrow. "We'll see."

Looking serious again, he leaned closer, squeezing my ankle. "Forgive me? I promise to cut back at work and pay more attention to you. To us."

I reached out, brushing the hair back from his face. Traced the shadows under his eyes. Exhaustion blanketed him. His working so much was about more than us. He was going to work himself to death if he didn't get a handle on it.

Not wanting to waste any more time fighting, I said, "I guess it depends on if you got me any General Tso's."

He grinned, then sat back and twisted, reaching behind him. Once he had what he needed, he presented me with chopsticks and a container of my favorite dish. "Guess I lucked out."

I took it from him and grabbed a bite with my chopsticks. "Yeah, you totally would've stayed in the dog house if you'd gotten me something lame like sweet and sour chicken."

"I got that, too."

"From the looks of it, you got one of everything."

He shrugged, not seeming a bit sorry. "Like I said, I didn't know what you liked." Glancing over at my empty ice cream container, he raised a brow. "And I was pretty sure what was on your menu for tonight."

"Don't be a snob. Ice cream is a perfectly acceptable meal replacement."

"Not tonight, it's not. I needed you to have more sustenance than sugar and cream. Especially for all the makeup sex we're gonna have later."

"Awfully sure of yourself, aren't you?"

He pulled an egg roll from a container, dipped it in sweet and sour sauce, and held his hand under it as he brought it to my lips, waiting for me to open. I obliged and took a bite, letting him feed me. I wouldn't admit it to him, but he'd been right—ice cream hadn't done shit for my hunger.

Wiping under the curve of my lip, he asked, "Am I wrong?"

No. He wasn't.

Instead of saying that, I lifted a shoulder and

plucked another bite from my carton. "I don't know…what's your fortune say, Mr. Know-It-All?"

With a quirk of his brow, he grabbed one of the fortune cookies, ripping open the packaging and breaking apart the cookie. "Happiness isn't an outside job, it's an inside job." He shot me a devilish grin, pinning me with eyes darkened with want. "I'm ready to do all the inside work you can give me if it makes you happy. Deep, wet, inside work."

Yeah, he was definitely getting some tonight. Fight be damned.

chapter eight

BRANDON

SPENDING ANOTHER WEEK in the heaven that was waking up with Gen, fucking her senseless before breakfast, working eight-hour days, hurrying home so I could chase her around the house all night, and giving her multiple orgasms, had sadly caught up with me. It was Saturday, and I'd already been at work for ten hours. The sun was still shining outside, but I was stuck in my office going over files and signing off on the updates my team had made.

I really wanted to be home with Gen.

Eighteen years of holding back, of the absolute bare minimum of feminine attention, had left me starved for it. And the fact that the person giving me the attention was my hot-as-fuck Genesis only made it worse. I craved her every minute of every day. Not just for her body, but for her laugh and smiles, her personality. Her.

I lived for the moments when we could finally settle down enough to be calm. We'd lie on the couch snuggled up together, and she'd tell me about her day or I'd tell her about mine. We'd talk about our future, our plans, the latest television show, random shit…anything and everything. It was the best kind of bliss. If only I didn't have to work so hard and spend so many hours away from her. I'd promised her I'd try harder to be home, but with the way Clark kept throwing potential clients my way…well, that was going to be more difficult than I'd hoped.

I organized a stack of contracts I needed to sign once the notary was in on Monday. The idea of popping in on Sunday while Genesis was working to finalize a few loose ends was just slipping through my mind when I heard a click from outside my office. I looked up to see the woman of the hour, the one who owned my heart and my mind, standing in the doorway.

"What are you doing here, baby?" I stood, smiling. She wore some sheer leggings under a sweatshirt that hung off her shoulder and all the way past her thighs. Casually hot was what I'd call it. Sexy. And yet, too much clothing in the way. Already, I could feel the burning need to rip the fabric from her body and get my hands on her flesh.

Gen shrugged and stepped inside, biting that plump, red lip of hers. Motherfucking red. "I got lonely. I wanted to pay you a visit."

"I thought you were working."

"I am." Her smile turned wicked. "Seems Harper

has another product she wants my opinion on. I figured I'd track you down so you can tell me what you think."

My cock was hard before she finished her sentence. Harper sent Gen home with lots of fun and interesting toys to try out. We already had an entire drawer of things we'd used on one another. I'd never had such an adventurous partner before, but I loved it. If the toy gave her pleasure, if I got to watch her face twist up as she came because of something I was doing, I was in. And she knew it.

"What sort of toy is it this time?"

"Oh, it's not a toy." She grinned and looked down, tugging the hem of her sweatshirt until it rose above her hips.

"Jesus, fuck." I fell back into my chair as she turned the corner of my desk, my eyes locked on lace and straps and skin. The leggings weren't really leggings—they were thigh-high stockings. Underneath that oversized sweatshirt was a black garter belt holding up the stockings and nothing else but bare pussy. My girl was naughty, and I was a very, very lucky man.

I spread my knees and leaned forward, crooking a finger in her direction as I kept my eyes locked between her legs. "C'mere. Let me get a closer look at this."

She inched between my legs, still smiling, looking at me like I was the sort of man who deserved to see such a goddess in something so fucking sexy. I didn't deserve it; not at all. But she thought I did, so I'd try. I'd try so fucking hard for her.

I ran a finger over the strap holding up her stockings. Bows. There were motherfucking bows. "This is very nice."

"It's a new line Harper's thinking about carrying. Do you like it?"

She pulled the sweatshirt higher, sort of prancing in a circle to give me the full show. I had to press my palm to my cock when I got the rear view. Her ass was on full display. Not a damn thing except two silky straps in my way. I couldn't resist. I reached out, one hand going to each cheek. Squeezing them before I leaned forward and bit her. Not too hard, just enough to test. To tease. She had to like it, because she groaned before reaching back to playfully knock my face away.

I gave that ripe, lush skin a tiny kiss before running my hands over it again. "Such a fucking perfect ass."

She looked over her shoulder, that seductress stare missing. Seeming almost…nervous. "She got in some new plugs, too. But I wasn't sure—I didn't know if—"

"Oh hell, Gen." I massaged her ass, then trailed my thumbs down between her thighs, teasing her pussy with light, soft strokes. "If that's what you want, I'm in. But we don't have to, especially not today. I can't be patient enough to try something that new today."

Unable to resist a second longer, I spun her around and tossed her pretty ass up on my desk. Work be damned. Papers fell to the floor, files scattering, but I didn't give a single fuck. My girl was here looking like pure sex in heels, and she made my mouth water. Paperwork could wait; I needed to make her scream.

"Lie back, baby." I unbuckled my belt and unfastened my pants, keeping my eyes on her. Gen leaned back on her elbows and spread her legs, so fucking inviting, but that wasn't the position I wanted her in. It might not be the time to try something as new as fucking her ass, but we could certainly try out a new position.

I grabbed her knees and held them together, dragging her ass to the edge. She yelped but didn't resist. In fact, she did a sort of wiggle as if she liked being manhandled.

A thought that made my hands clutch at her legs a little tighter. "You came here to get fucked, didn't you?"

"I came here *hoping* you'd fuck me. I wasn't sure if you'd be too busy…"

"I'll never be too busy for you. For this. I promise you that." I kept her legs together and placed her calves against one shoulder, forcing her to twist slightly to her side. Her pussy was almost hidden in this position, the pink, swollen lips barely peeking out from her thighs. It was as if she were teasing me, even though I was the one holding her.

"Fuck, that's so pretty." I grabbed my cock and dragged it through her lips, spreading her wetness with the tip. Purposely bumping her clit. "How can I work when your swollen, needy little pussy is out on display for me?"

"That was sort of the point—I was hoping you'd stop working. I've gotta look out for my man, remember?" She grinned up at me, suddenly all sweet and bubblegum cute. Not that I fell for that. She'd come here without real pants, without panties, looking for my cock. She gave me that innocent grin while her bare ass was on my desk and my cock was rubbing along her pussy. Such a naughty thing, my Gen.

"I want to fuck you, baby. Want to get you so wet, you drip on this old desk." I slid deep, groaning, biting her calf as she swallowed me up. "I want to have memories of you here. Want them to drive me crazy."

"That's only fair…I see you—us—everywhere I look at home."

I loved it when she called the house home. I definitely saw it as our home. "Is that what you want? You want to drive me so crazy I have to jack off right at my desk? Want me to have to come all silent and careful so no one knows how fucking obsessed I am with this pussy?"

She groaned and grabbed her tit, squeezing as her head lolled to the side. My horny fucking girl. I loved it when she got like this, all needy and demanding. There was nothing better than seeing her lose control, especially when I was the one pushing her to do it.

I thrust harder, practically growling as she panted and writhed beneath me. Already, she'd begun chanting my name and grabbing at my arms, a sure sign she was close. I'd learned her little body, had studied it. I knew her tells, and I worked hard to make sure she got off at least once every fucking time.

"C'mon, baby." I was dying to go deeper, so I

pulled her legs up a little higher to get a better angle. Gen dropped her head back, her mouth open in a silent scream as she hit that point of no return. "Fuck, yeah. Come, baby. Give it to me, let me feel you milk my cock."

A little more, just a few extra strokes, and I came with a growl that left my head spinning. This girl, this fucking girl, had ruined me. There was no one else, no one better, nothing I wanted more. And as I emptied inside her, as I shook and thrust and clung to her, I knew this was it for me. She was it for me. I just had to find a way to keep her.

"We made a mess," Gen said when we'd both calmed down enough to speak. Well, mostly. I was still older than her. My calm-down period was a bit longer.

I pressed my forehead to her chest while I caught my breath. Still shivering from the strongest orgasm of my life. "Yeah, we did. Thank fuck for that."

Gen wiggled under me, so I pulled back to give her room. My cock slid out of her pussy as she moved, and I grimaced at how cold it was. We needed to leave or else I'd be fucking her again as soon as I was able to. Maybe on the couch in the corner, or up against the windows looking out over the lake.

I tucked myself back into my pants, thinking over the possibilities on the way home to stop for a little outside action. I was a man obsessed, and happily so. "Give me a minute to clean up, and we can go home."

"I thought you needed to work."

"I was getting ready to leave when you showed

up. Besides, I'm not done with this outfit yet." I grabbed a few tissues from the dispenser on my desk and helped her clean up, kissing her shoulder as I did. "I can't wait to figure out how to get it off of you."

"I might not make it easy on you."

"I'm willing to work for it."

She smiled at me over her shoulder. That look, that happiness, gutted me. I wanted to tell her my plans right then. Wanted to tell her I loved her and hoped she'd stay with me. Wanted to put a fucking ring on her finger and show the world she was mine. I wanted the motherfucking fairy tale with her at the center of it, but the ogre ruined the moment.

"Brandon, old boy. I didn't expect—" Clark froze in the doorway, looking from me to Gen and back again. Gen tugged her sweatshirt down, making sure to cover herself, but the scene was pretty damning. Papers scattered and on the floor, Gen standing too close to me, both of us disheveled. He knew. He had to know.

I was screwed. "Clark. What are you doing here on a Saturday?"

"I think I should be asking you the same question."

"I was catching up on the McIntyre Steel paperwork. This is—" I froze, unable to think of the word to use. I wanted something more than girlfriend, something meaningful that explained the gravity and seriousness of our relationship, but I hadn't even told her how I felt yet. Hadn't asked her if she'd be my girlfriend. Hell, I didn't know if people still asked such things. I was at a loss, so I stumbled. "This is

Evie's friend."

I knew I'd fucked up the second the words left my lips. Evie's friend? Gen was more than that, so much more. She was my new world, my future, my love. She was everything to me, and by the set of her shoulders, I'd just hurt her. I hadn't even said her damn name. Fuck.

"Hello again, Mr. Wilkinson. We met briefly at Evie's graduation party. I know your son from school."

Clark's eyebrows practically jumped off his forehead. "You're in high school?"

"No, not anymore. I graduated with Evie and Brock."

"I see." Clark looked us over again, frowning. "Well, I guess I can leave you two to it. Brandon, I want you in my office first thing on Monday."

"Yes, sir."

"And perhaps you should clean up this mess so you can get back to going over contracts like you're paid to do." He eyed Genesis in a way that made the blood boil in my veins. "Too many distractions from work won't get you to that forty-eight percent ownership stake you've been wanting."

Distractions. Fuck, as if Genesis was something so trivial, so small. Work had become my distraction from her, and it was something I knew I'd need to deal with. But not yet—I wasn't ready. Unfortunately, Clark had just shoved me into oncoming traffic without any idea of how to get back to safety.

As soon as he walked out of the office, I reached for Genesis, trying to come up with something to say to fix things between us. Knowing nothing I said would work. "I'm sorry—"

Gen shoved my hands away, backing up until she was on the other side of the desk. "Sorry about what? The fact that you basically treated me like a whore you were ashamed of being caught with? Jesus, Brandon. I wasn't expecting a declaration, but you couldn't even use my name?"

Her distance sent ice through my veins. "Gen, please. It was a mistake. I wasn't thinking when he walked in, and I didn't know how to handle the situation."

"I'm not a situation to be handled. I'm a person. And you are an asshole."

She spun toward the door, and my heart dropped. There was no way I could let her go, no fucking way I could let her walk out the door without knowing how I felt about her.

"Gen, stop. Please. I know you're a person. Don't you think I know that?" I hurried after her, keeping distance between us because it seemed to be what she wanted even though I was dying to touch her. Grab her. Hold her to me. "Please believe me when I say I'm sorry. You're...you're everything to me."

"According to you, I'm just your daughter's friend." She walked out the door without looking back.

I followed her, unable not to. "Gen, stop. Come back and talk to me."

"You just lost every right you ever had to even attempt to tell me what to do. I thought I meant more to you than that. I thought what we had—"

Her voice cracked, and her shoulders shook as she took a deep breath before turning once more to face me. "I thought I was more than just a piece of ass to you."

The look on her face, the pain. It rocked me. Sent my heart and mind reeling in ways nothing else ever had. Not finding out I was going to be a father at just nineteen, not Evie's mom walking out of our lives a few short years later, not even learning my daughter and my best friend were together. Nothing in my life had prepared me for the level of hurt I'd caused Genesis.

"You are." I reached for her, unable not to. "You're so much more to me. I swear if you'd just give me time—"

She waved me off before turning her back on me once more. "Give you time? We've been here before, haven't we? Everything about us is new, and yet you've managed to let me down over and over again. I'm done."

The door to the parking lot slammed behind her, the sound sharp and final. That was it. One slip, one stupid mistake on my part, and I'd lost the most important thing in my life. I'd failed Gen, and I had no idea how to fix that.

Or if I ever could.

chapter nine

GENESIS

I SWIPED AT the tears as they fell on my drive ho— I cut off my thoughts before the word could even finish going through my mind and internally cursed myself for having started to think of Brandon's place as home. After mere weeks, I'd already begun to think of it as mine. Ours.

Turned out it had all been one-sided.

The beautiful neighborhood he lived in blurred past as I sped down the street. Bet they didn't see a lot of screeching, fifteen-year-old Hondas in these parts. I hoped I left tire marks on his pristine driveway, just a little reminder of how he'd burned me.

It took me three tries before I could fit the key into the lock, then push the front door open. The peaceful feeling I'd been getting for the past week as

I'd walked into the house was still there, echoing in my heart, and I hated it. I *hated* it.

I hated that he'd made me feel safe and happy and wanted and…loved. That bastard had made me feel loved, all the while thinking I was nothing more than just a pussy to fuck.

Well, fuck him and this perfect house and this perfect life that I didn't need. That I'd never thought I wanted. That I'd never fit into.

I tore through the house like a windstorm, picking up discarded pieces of myself everywhere I turned. A throw blanket I'd brought over from my apartment, the bags of goodies from Sin that Harper had been sending home with me left and right. The fresh flowers I'd picked up at the farmer's market got plucked from the too-fancy vase and tossed in the trash.

The worst part of the house would be Brandon's room, but there was no avoiding it. I told myself not to look around as I walked inside, hoping if I didn't look, I wouldn't be reminded of everything. Of course, that hope was in vain. Even with my eyes closed, I could remember every second of the past two weeks—God, had it really only been *weeks?*— we'd spent in there. When we'd lain in bed, watching a marathon of *Gilmore Girls* just because he knew it made me happy. When we'd sat on the floor, sharing a pizza and playing a silly game of Truth or Dare. When I'd fallen asleep before he'd gotten home, and he'd woken me up with kisses along the length of my spine…

With tears in my eyes, I snatched my pillow off the bed and tucked it to my chest, hating that it still smelled like him. I straightened my spine and went into his attached bathroom, grabbing my disposable toothbrush and chucking it in the trash can. Stupid, maybe, but I'd be damned if I was going to leave even a trace of myself in this house once I walked out.

Thank God Evie didn't live here anymore. I had no idea what I'd do if I had to walk into this place to see her.

Just the thought of my best friend made me pause in the act of stuffing my bag full of clothes. Thankfully, she'd been otherwise occupied these past weeks, too engrossed in her new relationship with Nate to pay me much mind. She had noticed something different, though, but I'd been avoiding her prodding questions. Brandon and I had talked about when would be a good time to tell her, and he'd thought it'd be a better idea to wait just a bit.

Apparently, he had no interest at all in telling her—or anyone—and instead was content to let me be a dirty secret he was ashamed of.

Once my bag was packed to the brim with clothes and toiletries, I hauled everything downstairs, intent on getting out of there as soon as fucking possible. No doubt my mom would be worried I was staying at the apartment by myself, but she'd just have to deal. She was getting stronger every day, her recovery proceeding much faster than the doctors had anticipated, so she'd be home in no time. But even if her progress hadn't been going in that direction, there was no way I'd be able to stay in this house another day, whether it was my mom's wishes or not.

I thought it'd been different with Brandon, but it turned out he was just like every other guy. All he saw in me was a pair of tits and a nice ass. He couldn't even bother to give my name when he'd introduced me. Like I was nothing to him—a nobody. I was simply an extension of his daughter.

The tears came again, burning my eyes as I jogged down the stairs, which pissed me off. And the anger roaring through my veins only served to make me cry harder. I put myself in this position, and as much as I wanted to point the finger at Brandon for being a total and complete ass, I really only had myself to blame. The hole in my chest, the ache in my stomach—those things were exactly why I'd always bailed before sex got too deep. If I ran first, that meant I didn't give them the chance to do it to me.

I was nearly at the bottom of the stairs, just steps from the front door, when it swung open, causing me to freeze in my descent while praying it was anyone but the aforementioned ass.

"Dad?" Evie called as she poked her head in, her gaze sweeping the entryway as she shut the door behind her. When she looked in my direction, she startled, her eyes going wide. And then she took in my disheveled appearance, the tear tracks down my face, and her lips turned down in a frown. "Gen? What's wrong? Is your mom all right?"

"Mom's fine," I croaked, my voice hoarse from withheld—and not so withheld—tears.

"Then what's—"

The door flew open behind her, making both of us jump, a squeak leaving my lips. Brandon came rushing in, his face stricken and panicked as he surveyed the entryway. "Genesis!"

"What the—" Evie started, dividing a look between her father and me.

Not able to stand there another minute, and certainly not able to stay in the presence of the man who'd just stomped all over my heart, I climbed down the rest of the stairs with the intention of heading straight out the still-open front door.

"Evie, I'll call you later, okay?" I said as I passed her.

"Umm…Dad?"

"Not now." Brandon hardly gave Evie a passing glance as he rushed past until he stood in front of me. "Gen, please. Give me a chance to apologize."

"Not interested. Your words have already done enough damage today. And I think I've had all of your sorries I can stomach."

He reached toward me, but something in my stiff as fuck body language must have alerted him now wasn't a time to touch, and he let his hand drop to his side. "Gen, please. Listen to me. I'm sorry. I am so fucking sorry for not introducing you as my—"

"Wait a second," Evie said, her gaze narrowed as she pointed a finger between her dad and me. "What's happening here?"

"What's happening here is your dad is an asshole." I turned my attention to Brandon. "Go ahead, Brandon.

Fill your daughter in if you're so keen on me listening to your apology."

Brandon didn't take his eyes off me as he said, "What's happening here is that I fucked up completely by not shouting from the rooftops how lucky I am to have Gen be mine. What's happening here is the woman I've fallen completely, utterly in love with didn't know how much she meant to me. That's my fault. I screwed up. But I want to make it right. I want to do better. I want you, Gen. I'll do anything if you'll just give me a second chance."

I wanted to believe him. God, did I want to. The sincerity of his words and the way he looked at me were enough to cause me pause. His stare was weighted, like he was trying to soak in every inch in case I actually walked away.

But all I could think about was that sinking feeling in my gut when he'd introduced me as Evie's friend. When he'd brushed our relationship—brushed *me*— under the rug in the face of public scrutiny. Not to mention all of his broken promises.

"I keep remembering how you made me feel in your office. You made me feel *replaceable*. Worse— you made me feel like I'd never had a place with you at all."

"I know, and if I could go back to that moment, I'd tell Clark exactly who you are to me."

"And what happens when he finds out? I heard every word he didn't say… Are you willing to gamble your job for this?"

"Yes."

"That's it? Yes? After how hard you worked for everything, you expect me to believe you'd give it up just for—"

"For everything I have ever wanted." He reached for me again, this time not stopping until my hand was in his, his thumb rubbing circles along the back. "I would gladly give up anything for you because nothing—not my job, my money, my house—nothing means more to me right now than you do. I know I haven't shown you that, and I know I've got a lot of ground to make up with you, but I'll do it. I'll work every day to make sure you know exactly what you mean to me and how important you are in my life. Just…give me the chance to fix this."

"Holy shit," Evie said.

Her words barely registered because I couldn't tear my attention away from Brandon, wanting so desperately to believe every word he said. "Do you mean it?"

"Every word. I'll call Clark right now and tell him about us. Shit, I'll call him and tell him to buy me out instead. Let Brock have my half of the company—I'm done working my life away. And then I'll take you to Nonno Pino's for that dinner I promised you that I missed, and I'll kiss you in front of the dining room so everyone knows you're mine. Hell, I'll buy out the billboard by the ferry dock so the whole damn town knows. Anything for you." With a tug, he pulled me closer and ran a finger down the length of my cheek before tracing the seam of my lips. "You are my everything, Genesis."

I leaned into his touch, unable to help myself. Despite his words in the office, I still felt this overwhelming pull toward him. And even though all my past experience was warning me away, my heart was begging me to stay. To accept his words for what I knew they were—the truth. "If you ever make me feel like that again, I'll cut off your dick and feed it to you."

"Won't happen, and not just because of your threat, though that's pretty motivational."

"Yeah," Evie said, bringing my attention away from Brandon, "you lost me at any discussion of my dad's dick." She stepped up to me, engulfing me in her arms. I tried to reciprocate, but Brandon held steadfast to my hand, only allowing me to give her a one-armed hug. Pulling back, she gripped me by the shoulders. "Call me later. I'm going to need the details, minus anything to do with my dad's dick." She cringed even as the words came out of her mouth.

"I'll call you," I promised, knowing I had weeks of emotions and buildup to fill her in on.

"And you," Evie turned to her dad, pushing a pointed finger into his chest. "I expect an explanation of what's going on here."

Brandon shrugged and smiled, looking more relaxed than I'd ever seen him. "I'm in love with your best friend, and I'm quitting my job to show her how much."

"Oh." Evie glanced between the two of us, and then understanding came over her face as she gave me a small smile before turning her attention to her dad. "Well then. Try not to fuck it up."

"I'll do my best."

The door closed and I assumed she left, but I couldn't take my eyes off Brandon. Couldn't believe he'd said those words. And not just to me, but in front of his daughter. Instead of telling him how much that meant to me, how much I loved him back, all that came out was, "I can't believe you told her that before you told me."

Before Brandon could respond, his cell phone rang. He pulled it out of his pocket and glanced at the screen, then back at me. "It's Clark."

"Um…we're kind of in the middle of something here…"

He grabbed my hand and squeezed, his eyes imploring me to be patient as he put the phone to his ear. "Hey, Clark, it's not a good time." He paused, the sounds of a response coming from his phone. "No. I'm not working more this weekend. I need time with my—"

Pulling his phone away from his mouth, he muffled the speaker against the material of his shirt. "I haven't had a girlfriend since Evie's mom, so I'm hopelessly lost on a lot of this, but in my day, we asked girls to be our girlfriends."

"Oh my God, you're so old," I whispered, but I couldn't stop the giggle that burst from my lips. Nor could I tamp down the butterflies that had erupted in my stomach at his words.

"I know. You seem to love to remind me of that." He grinned again, inching closer, leaning down to make the moment ours. "I'm way too old for you, but that's not going to stop me from wanting you. So, will you be my girlfriend?"

Pushing up on my tiptoes, I let my lips rest against his. "If you hang up that phone as soon as humanly possible and take me upstairs..."

He gave me a quick kiss, then brought the phone back to his ear. "Clark. Yeah, sorry about that. I'm spending the weekend with my girlfriend. You met her today. Genesis. Right. I think a chat first thing Monday is long overdue."

He pressed the end button on his screen before turning off his phone and tossing it on the entryway table. "Done. Now I think you said something about going upstairs?"

Before I could answer, he ducked down and lifted me over his shoulder, causing me to drop everything at his feet.

"Brandon!" I yelped and fisted his shirt as he spun us around and took off up the stairs with a slap to my ass. "Wow, for an old man, you sure can book it," I said around a laugh.

He growled and turned his head, sinking his teeth into my hip. "You're sure mouthy for someone who's gonna be riding my cock for the foreseeable future."

Obviously a man on a mission, he didn't stop until he had me on my back, sprawled out on his bed.

Then the amazing torture began.

He was slow this time, like he was trying to worship me through brushes of his lips and caresses of his fingers. With careful hands, he stripped me of my sweatshirt, then the thigh highs and garter belt, his mouth mapping every inch of skin he revealed.

"This is sexy as hell, but I want you naked. I just want *you* right now." He pressed a kiss to my hip, glancing up at me. "Promise you'll wear it for me again?"

"Only if you're good."

With a wicked smile, he pushed my legs apart and settled between them, his breaths brushing against my pussy with every word. "You want me to be good to you with my mouth or my cock? Or maybe you want both?"

He didn't wait for me to answer—he wouldn't need to because he knew exactly how much I loved both. He licked a long path up the length of my slit, his tongue flicking against my clit, sending shockwaves through my body.

With a groan, I sank my fingers into his hair. "God, that's good."

"Just good? I'm going to make you ride my tongue until I'm not just good anymore." He licked a warm, wet trail all around my clit then zeroed in again. Flicking, sucking, and teasing as he slid his fingers inside of me.

What started off unhurried turned feverish. He always got like this when he tasted me. He'd get so worked up that he'd slam me straight into my orgasm before taking me rough and hard. Then, when it was all over and he was holding me in his arms, he'd apologize for fucking me so hard and promise to slow down next time. But I loved it. I loved that he started out with the intention of being sweet. How he wanted to make love to me, but once he got a single taste, he turned into a starving man and my body was his last meal.

With the focused attention of his tongue on my clit and three fingers pumping in and out of me, he hurled me over the edge of my release before I even knew it was upon me. I couldn't do anything but clutch his shoulders and chant his name as I came against his mouth.

"You're going to be so sloppy wet when I get inside you," he said as he crawled up my body, taking time to swipe his tongue around my belly button, along the underside of one of my breasts, between the valley between them. And then he was above me, settling between my legs, and sliding home.

I dug my nails into his back, wrapping my legs around his hips and encouraging him with my heels pressing into his ass. "Feels so good."

He paused in his thrusts, pushing deep and rotating his hips. "It's not all this, you know. It's not just sex for me."

I stared up at him, at the honesty shining through in his eyes. "It's not for me either."

"I meant what I said, even if it wasn't necessarily directed your way. I love you, Genesis, and I promise to do whatever it takes to make you happy." He dropped his head and nipped my chin, licking a trail along my jaw until his lips rested against my ear. "Even if that means taking one for the team and fucking this luscious ass of yours."

My laughter was cut off as he began fucking me in earnest, the rapid staccato of our hips the only symphony I wanted to hear for the rest of my life. With whispered words of all the things he wanted to spend the next fifty years doing to me, he pushed me closer and closer to the edge. All I could do was cling to his shoulders, attempting to meet his hips thrust for thrust.

When I came, it was with the force of a tsunami, Brandon rocking me through my orgasm even as he found his own release.

As he settled his weight on me, pressing a kiss to my sweat-slicked shoulder, I knew this was it for me. I'd never get tired of being with this man—of laughing and talking and fucking. Of *loving*. While I'd never given much thought to where I wanted to be in ten or twenty years, I just always assumed I'd know it when it came along.

I'd been right.

epilogue
BRANDON

"BRANDON."

I glanced up at the familiar voice, smiling when I saw my cousin striding toward me. "Josh. How are things?"

"Good, man. Good. What're you doing at the coffee shop in the middle of the day?"

I nearly laughed. He was right to question me. For close to twenty years, I'd spent every waking moment tied to a desk, focused first on my education then on the glory of a good career instead of a good life. I'd been an idiot, but thankfully, Gen made sure I knew that and kept me from sliding into old habits.

"I was meeting a client about one of the empty storefronts on Main Street. Figured I'd finalize my notes here before heading home."

"So it's true? You left Wilkinson Properties?"

"I did," I said with a shrug. "Life's too short not to take advantage of every second."

"I can't believe you gave all that up." He frowned. "Is the other rumor true, as well? You're dating Genesis McKay?"

My smile grew, the thought of my Gen waiting for me making me itch to head home. "She's the best thing that's ever happened to me, outside of my daughter."

He nodded, seeming distracted. "Good for you, Brandon. I don't think I would—"

"You would. For the right woman, you would give up just about anything." I nodded across the street, where his nanny stood holding the hand of his son as they laughed about something in a store window. "Looks like your entourage is waiting."

"Yeah." He stared across the street, something close to yearning on his face. It was too hard to tell whether he was looking at his son or his young, pretty nanny.

"You should go," I said, figuring that was the right thing for him to do no matter which of the two he was staring at. "I'm heading home. Gen wants to go to the mainland for dinner tonight, and I am more than happy to oblige her."

Josh turned back, a weak smile on his face. "You're happy, then? Even with the age difference and all the gossip?"

I shrugged, tossing my notebook into my bag. "I'm thrilled. And anyone who wants to talk shit about me and Gen can fuck right off. This isn't some secret, naughty affair. I love her. I'm going to marry her someday. End of story."

"I'm thrilled for you. Really." He slapped me on the shoulder. Before he could speak again, Bailey yelled his name from across the street. He spun immediately, his lips turning up in a much stronger smile when she waved to him. No wonder he was so interested in Gen and me. Josh had the hots for the nanny. "I should go."

I chuckled and shook my head. "Yeah, you should. You should also pull your head out of your ass."

"What?"

"Never mind." I waved across the street. "Hi, Max. Good to see you, Bailey."

They waved back, and I slapped a hand down on Josh's shoulder. "Beautiful family."

He looked back across the street, and this time, I knew he wasn't looking at his son. "Yeah, it is."

The tone of his voice reminded me of my own when I spoke of Gen, the reverence even I could hear. Thank fuck we'd worked things out and were still together. Just the thought, the reminder of how I'd almost let her slip through my fingers, was enough to make my feet move.

"See you Tuesday, Josh."

"Tuesday?"

"Release day for Lara McKay. I'm coming with Gen to help get her mom settled at her new place."

"Oh, right. Yeah. See you then."

I was in my car and pulling out into ferry traffic seconds later. The problem with living on an island was there were only so many ways on or off. On the south end, you had the ferry traffic; on the west, the bridge. Both caused far more congestion than you'd think possible.

I worked my way through the clogged business district until I bypassed the bridge and hit the road that ringed the island before turning north. If I hurried, I could be home in fifteen minutes. If I really hurried, I could already be inside Gen in that same amount of time.

Thank fuck for fast cars.

But when I strolled into the foyer and yelled for Gen, no one answered. I set my bag down and walked through the downstairs, seeing all the little signs of her. A hair tie on the foyer table, her shoes next to the door, a half-empty bottle of lemonade on the kitchen counter. Her presence permeated every inch of my big, cold house, bringing warmth to the place. And I loved it.

I found Gen in the family room. She'd built a sort of tent out of blankets she'd draped across the couch and side chair. She was curled around a pillow inside it, her skimpy shorts riding up enough to show off the fleshy curve of her ass, her leg hitched over the blanket covering the floor. Her lips were slightly parted, her face clean of any makeup, and her hair piled high on top of her head. Irresistible, and so fucking beautiful she made my chest hurt.

Unable to wait a minute longer, I tugged off my tie and shirt, dropped my pants and let my boxers fall to the floor. We still had a few hours before we needed to leave for dinner. Might as well spend them in my favorite way possible. True, Gen was only practically naked—which was not nearly naked enough—but I could fix that.

I crawled into her little blanket fort and tugged the side down, cocooning us inside. The closeness, the shadows—they reminded me of that first night on the couch in this same room. The way Gen had teased me, how I'd pulled her into my lap. That first orgasm I'd given her. There'd been many more since—dozens more—but that one meant something to me. It was our start, our beginning, and though the road had been a little rocky afterward, we'd navigated it together. And now, she was mine.

Gen jerked then moaned as my hand ran up under her tank top to cup her breast. I leaned over her, pressing my chest to her back and kissing along her neck, letting her feel how hard I was for her. How much I wanted her.

"You're half naked on the floor," I whispered before biting her earlobe gently. "Something you need?"

"Yeah, I was planning to get that dildo Harper sent me home with." She arched into me, pulling me closer, almost forcing my hand down her body. "But I guess you'll do…"

"I can leave you to it," I said, even though there was no way I could peel myself away from her now. She knew it, too. Her light chuckle was a sure sign of it. "I could always get that new toy and use it on you if you'd rather."

"Maybe tonight. Now give me what I want."

Gen reached behind me, palming my ass to pull me closer.

"So damn bossy." I gave in and rolled, positioning her on her stomach, and dragged her skimpy panties down her legs as she tugged off her tank top. When I had her bare, I worked a thigh between hers, angled my hips to push my cock against her, and I rocked. She groaned and tried to move, but I had her pinned, teasing her with the length of my cock running along her slit while my fingers focused on her clit.

"Brandon," she moaned, her fingers clutching the blanket below her.

"I've got you, baby," I said, rolling my hips into hers. Stretching out on her back to keep her in place. "Spread your legs a little so I can show you. So I can make you come on my cock. No toys, just me and you."

Gen groaned and grabbed my wrist, as if making sure I couldn't get away. Not that I'd try. When you had a girl like Genesis in your heart and your bed, there was no escaping her. No use trying. She was perfect for me—witty and fun and sexy in a way that knocked me on my ass several times a day. And as I slid inside her, as she sighed and rocked and whispered my name, I knew she was it for me. There was no one better, no one who understood me as well, no one else.

She was my everything, and she always would be.

also available from

TEMPERANCE FALLS

She's completely off limits

In my eyes—and those of every woman on Temperance Falls—Doctor Josh Hutton is the ultimate catch: single dad, handsome surgeon, and lonely widower all rolled into one. He's also my boss. I shouldn't want to take our relationship from professional to personal, but I ache thinking about even one night in his bed.

His control is slipping

I know better than to lust after Bailey, but that doesn't stop me from doing it. She's my employee, the person who cares for my son when I can't, which only makes the dirty thoughts I have about her even more inappropriate. But she's also a beautiful, sexy woman living under my roof, and that temptation is hard to resist. A door left ajar and a breathy moan is all it takes. One night of pushed boundaries, and all my rules go out the window.

about the author

London Hale is the combined pen name of writing besties Ellis Leigh and Brighton Walsh. Between them, they've published more than thirty books in the contemporary romance, paranormal romance, and romantic suspense genres. Ellis is a *USA Today* bestselling author who loves coffee, thinks green Skittles are the best, and prefers to stay in every weekend. Brighton is multi-published with Berkley, St. Martin's Press, and Carina Press. She hates coffee, thinks green Skittles are the work of the devil, and has never heard of a party she didn't want to attend. Don't ask how they became such good friends or work so well together—they still haven't figured it out themselves.

www.londonhale.com

www.ingramcontent.com/pod-product-compliance
Lightning Source LLC
Chambersburg PA
CBHW032047180726
48284CB00004B/1218